Dispersing the Clouds of Temptation

DISPERSING THE CLOUDS OF
TEMPTATION

Turning Away from Weakness of Will
and Turning towards the Sun

Brian Lightbody

PICKWICK *Publications* · Eugene, Oregon

DISPERSING THE CLOUDS OF TEMPTATION
Turning Away from Weakness of Will and Turning towards the Sun

Pickwick Publications
An Imprint of Wipf and Stock Publishers
199 W. 8th Ave., Suite 3
Eugene, OR 97401

www.wipfandstock.com

ISBN 13: 978-1-61097-074-7

Cataloguing-in-Publication Data

Lightbody, Brian

    Dispersing the clouds of temptation : turning away from weakness of will and turning towards the sun / Brian Lightbody

    xiv + 142 p. ; 23 cm. Includes bibliographical references and index.

    ISBN 13: 978-1-61097-074-7

    1. Plato. 2. Akrasia. 3. Will. 4. Compulsive behavior. 5. Volition. 6. Philosophy, Ancient. I. Title.

B395 L54 2015

Manufactured in the U.S.A.   04/16/2015

Contents

Preface

THE CARTOON, "DONALD DUCK'S Better Self" (1938) depicts a conflict with which we as humans are all too familiar. The cartoon begins with Donald being awakened by his wind-up alarm clock. An angel, representing Donald's better self, gently extols Donald to get up. But another Donald, this time dressed up as a devil and clearly representing Donald's weaker self, coaxes Donald to fall back to sleep. Eventually Donald gets up to go to school, thanks to the strong exhortations by "Angel Donald" and proceeds to take the road to the schoolhouse. Nevertheless, it is clear that Donald goes to school unwillingly: his heart is not in it. "Devil Donald" senses Donald's unwillingness, and proceeds to tempt Donald away from the path that is clearly in Donald's best interest. The Devil Donald takes advantage of Donald's "weak will" and convinces Donald to fish instead of going to school. Later, Devil Donald capitalizes on Donald's weakened state of will and cajoles Donald to try smoking by giving him a pipe. Eventually, the angel and devil battle presumably for the soul and therefore future direction of Donald. The angel wins and Donald goes off to school.

The ideas raised by the cartoon are immediately understood and obvious, even to young children. Our sense of self, at least at times, is a deeply furrowed entity: we feel conflicted between what we ought to do and what we desire to do. What's more, existing in such a state, where we feel torn, conflicted, divided, is often accompanied with a sense of negative affectation—in such states, especially if prolonged, we feel depressed, inauthentic, alienated, and weak-willed.

How can we be made whole? How do we conquer this weaker self that gives in too readily to temptation? The present book attempts to answer these and other questions. Interestingly, the overall solution presented in the work is one that is already depicted toward the end of "Donald's Better

Self." When Donald finally decides to go off to school, the Angel Donald is no longer distinguishable from Donald himself. Angel and Donald become one: the cartoon shows how they become a singular fused entity. Philosophers from Plato to Aristotle to Harry Frankfurt have attempted to show how full and complete identification with the one's true self is possible. Inspired by these philosophers, the present work is yet another effort in this tradition. Like them, I hope to inspire readers to discover and become their true destinies.

Acknowledgments

I WOULD LIKE TO thank the editorial team at Wipf and Stock and, of course, my students and colleagues at Brock University.

Introduction

HAVE YOU EVER MADE a resolution? Have you ever failed to follow through on it? If you have then some might consider you weak-willed—and you might be inclined to agree. But should you? What is weakness of will? Is weakness of will a disposition, a propensity, a mar on the powers of will? Or is it a descriptive term that denotes a person who acts against his better judgment? Or is it perhaps a misnomer? Is it a simply a misunderstanding; one who fails to follow through on a resolution is not weak-willed, but ignorant. The following book addresses these and other related questions.

This work seeks to examine the very essence of weakness of will. The goal, in this case, as is true for most areas of philosophy, is to "reach bottom." To reach bottom in philosophical investigations often entails discovering the fundamental and irreducible components that comprise the idea being investigated. My understanding of reaching bottom, though, is not entirely congruent with this traditional practice; it involves much more than a conceptual analysis of a given notion. In sum, I argue that one must understand weakness of will as best one can from two angles: conceptually and affectively. Only when this dual analysis is complete can one begin to understand and cure weakness of will.

I begin my analysis by examining the ancient Greek term for weakness of will: *akrasia*. I prefer to investigate the idea of *akrasia* to that of weakness of will, because such a notion, conceptually speaking, seems less metaphysically ornate than the term "weakness of will" and, therefore, makes the goal of reaching bottom somewhat easier. I then examine *akrasia* from four interpolated questions, which, if successfully answered, will come to provide a sufficient understanding of the term. After examining these four questions in considerable detail, I turn to investigate the affective attitudes that are often attached to weak-willed actions. I conclude chapter one by outlining what I believe a successful inquiry regarding *akrasia,* as both a notion and feeling, would look like.

Chapter two, in some ways, could be construed as a digression, but this would be a serious mistake. In this chapter I examine what is perhaps one of the strongest pieces of writing to deny the very existence of weakness of will: Plato's *Protagoras.* It is important to examine Socrates' arguments against the very possibility of *akrasia* because if his arguments are sound then the task of investigating weakness of will would be for nought. I examine Socrates' argument against the very existence of *akrasia* in considerable detail.

Socrates' overall argument is not without flaws. I expose these flaws and demonstrate that at some point Plato must have become aware of these problems too as his position begins to shift during the course of his writing. I end the chapter by marking this shift of position on *akrasia* in *Meno. Meno* is the key to understanding Plato's later position on *akrasia* as presented in his middle works.[1]

In chapter three, I turn to analyzing Plato's more mature understanding of such notions as movement (why we act as we do), *akrasia,* and the soul. I begin my analysis with *Phaedo* before moving to examine *Symposium.* I then provide an analysis of Plato's well-known tripartite model of the soul as first evinced in book IV of *Republic.* In *Republic,* Plato no longer denies the existence of *akrasia* as he did in *Protagoras.* Indeed he recognizes that reason, broadly construed, can indeed be overpowered by desire—an idea that is considered incoherent in *Protagoras.* I then examine Plato's contrary model to weakness of will: the soul as one's best friend. To be one's own best friend is to be a soul without strife: the soul's parts, including (both the rational and irrational divisions) live together in perfect harmony.

In chapter four, I explore the tools Plato counsels us to use in order to maintain a state of concordance with all aspects of our soul. Moreover, I demonstrate that the cave analogy, as depicted in Book VII of *Republic,* substantiates the initial affective conception of *akrasia* I outlined in chapter one. I argue that overcoming weakness of will is accomplished through a double turn: one turns towards virtue and simultaneously turns away from vice. In turning towards virtue, a subject is inspired to reach some ideal. In turning away from vice, one is pushed to overcome the shame or feeling of deep dissatisfaction that one has come to associate with oneself.

1. The "middle works" of Plato denote the dialogues that were written by Plato in the middle period of his writing career. They typically focus on metaphysical and epistemological themes.

In the concluding chapter, I distill the lessons learned from the previous chapters. I demonstrate that the true roots for self-transformation come both from "below" and from "above": though effective upbuilding resolutions must be well-considered intentions, they are just as much products of highly-charged emotional groundswells. Self-approbation is possible provided that one can transmute one's affective, emotional states into principles for joyful self-ownership.

It is my hope that by exploring weakness of will in this affective way, a new and seminal vein of inquiry has been opened for greater exploration. Weakness of will or again *akrasia* (being without power or rule) is a real phenomenon: it defines a possible relationship that we may have to the self. But as I hope to show, it need not define us—transformation is possible. As I try to demonstrate (by revealing the conceptual and affective underpinnings of weakness of will) we can improve the relationship we have to ourselves only if we perform the hard work of identifying the push and pull forces that disperse the clouds of temptation allowing all of us to ascend towards the Sun.[2]

2. The Sun is an analogue for the Good in Plato's most celebrated and widely read work, *Republic*. Here I am using it as a metaphor to demonstrate the ideal relationship we instinctively seek to create to ourselves.

Chapter One

What is Weakness of Will?

PHILOSOPHERS BEGIN A PHILOSOPHICAL investigation by asking questions. The investigation that is the subject matter of the present book is no different. However, all philosophical questions serve to guide subsequent query. This point seems obvious and perhaps trivial to some, but it will have significant bearing on our investigation as will be seen. For example, questions such as: "What is Being?" Or "What is Knowledge?" seem to be basic starting points for the philosophical areas of metaphysics and epistemology respectively. Indeed, it is difficult to conceive of a more basic foundation from which to investigate these fields of philosophic inquiry. Such questions, furthermore, seem to not only be elementary, but integral to the very formation of each area. For if these questions make sense then the area of philosophy that is in question, unfolds almost naturally.

Indeed, we might even call such queries "classic Socratic questions" for they have the bare structure of the kind of questions Socrates asks in the early Platonic dialogues (e.g., *Protagoras, Laches, Euthyprho,* etc.) The above two questions have the same basic structure: they ask what is the essence of some thing? Richard Robinson, a highly respected Platonic scholar, called such questions, "What is X?" questions and claims that this sort of questioning is indicative of an *aporetic* Platonic dialogue: a type of dialogue that belongs to Plato's early period of writing and one, moreover, characterized by a failure of the interlocutors of the dialogue to come to any definitive conclusion or answer regarding some philosophical question.[1]

1. See Robinson's *Plato's Early Dialectic,* chapter 5. The early Platonic dialogues are

For example, in *Euthyphro*, Socrates asks Euthyphro, a temple priest, "What is Piety?" Euthyphro attempts to answer Socrates' question—though failing miserably in the process—by providing a definition that would serve to explain all instances of pious reverence.[2] Socratic questions try to get at the essence of some concept by defining it. Although Socrates is not successful in the early dialogues in eliciting such an answer, the method, called elenchus, is still important and has become a hallmark of philosophic inquiry ever since.[3]

The idea behind Socrates' method is to demonstrate that either (a) some idea is conceptually contained within a larger genus or (b) to show that the concept is a unique combination of two more basic and immediately knowable ideas. Let's concretize the above point by providing an example. Let us investigate the question "What is knowledge?" The first step of the investigation would require that we define what knowledge is. This definition would seek to arrive at the essence for all examples of knowledge. We would then proceed to answer this question by demonstrating how one might satisfy the necessary conditions for the answer. By satisfying the necessary conditions needed to acquire knowledge, we would then and only then be able to provide a sufficient response to the "What is knowledge?" question as well as the related question, "How may we attain it?" Unfortunately, not all approaches to philosophical questions appear this simple and straightforward.

Continuing with this line of inquiry, one might claim that to define knowledge requires, at the very least, a three-part analysis. In *Theaetetus*, Plato, via the character Theaetetus, provides his infamous tripartite definition of knowledge. He writes: "He said that it [knowledge] is a true judgment with an account."[4] In effect, Plato evinces that knowledge is comprised of three components: a belief, the justification for this belief, and the truth of the belief in question. Thus, an answer to the singular question: "What

---

characterized by failure: the interlocutors do not arrive at a definition for the idea they are pursuing. Instead, such dialogues conclude in *aporia* (an impasse). Socratic questions also serve as handy touchstones in determining whether one is reading an early, middle, or late dialogue.

2. Robinson argues that Plato soon abandoned this frame for philosophical questioning by asking a different type of question in the middle dialogues, namely, the "Is X Y?" question.

3. See Vlastos, "Socratic Elenchus."

4. Plato, *Theaetetus*, (201d), 223.

is knowledge?" Now involves three: "What is belief?" "What is truth?" and "What is justification?"

To answer each of these questions is to get closer to the overall answer that one initially sought. There is a clear path, so to speak, to the destination of the query. To be certain, the destination, as the annals of Western philosophy show, is still difficult to reach. Such a mapping of the destination point does not make the journey any easier. Each of the above questions will have their own sub-questions and so on. Although there are many branches to each of these paths and some of these branches may lead to dead-ends, still, there is at least a firm understanding of where one needs to go; there is a sense that one is inching closer and closer to the desired endpoint.

This is not the case with the above question: "What is weakness of will?" For infused within this seemingly basic question are questionable, contestable, and indeed problematic conceptual frameworks which, if accepted as elementary, or indubitable starting points, serve to direct, uncritically, and indeed perhaps even skew, unknowingly, any subsequent inquiry founded thereon. There is "something more" that needs to be explored as regards this question than the questions put forward above. They appear in the parlance of the logical positivists to have the same logical form as the above question concerning knowledge, but when the grammatical garb is removed, the logical form of this question takes on a whole new appearance.[5]

What's more, such questions (e.g. "What is weakness of will?") when uncritically assumed to be basic or self-grounded naturally spill over— much like boiling water left in a pot that has been unattended—into other fields, making a mess of everything. For example, the problem of weakness of will has been taken up by epistemologists. Some epistemologists have argued that the solution to the justification question (the J question) or "When is a subject justified in believing some proposition?" requires a virtuous component.[6] Such scholars support this contention by arguing for two points: (1) the act of investigating is not a purely epistemic matter. It is not cognitively self-contained; there is leakage. For to investigate any given area or matter of inquiry presupposes that there is a desire on the part of some subject to perform this investigation and not some other. Thus, investigations are not value neutral: there is an agenda regarding the very purpose of the investigation. It is in the very nature of an investigation to be

5. See Ayer, *Language, Truth and Logic.*
6. See Zagzebski, *Virtues of the Mind.*

shot through with interest, broadly construed.[7] (2) Even if we restrict ourselves to mere fact acquisition, it is clear that facts, which are propositional attitudes believed to be true, are not value neutral either. For believing itself is an action and therefore pertains to the will of an agent. An agent must decide whether he or she desires to pursue some object of investigation. No inquiry could begin without some epistemic desire of some agent to know something about some object.

Justificatory failure might occur, so this theory goes, not because the subject lacks the required cognitive capacities to know p, where p stands in place for some proposition, some statement taken to be true, but because he lacks the *willpower* to believe p to be true. The individual is weak-willed, but not necessarily weak-minded: he understands both the evidence that is required along with the amount of such evidence needed in order to have sufficient justification to believe in some statement, yet he still fails to believe because he does not wish the statement to be true.[8] He may even believe some statement such as: "If another rational agent were presented with the same evidence, E, which I just examined, he would conclude P and therefore believe P, but I cannot." If this line of reasoning is a live option, then scholars, who self-identify as virtue epistemologists, argue that some other component other than belief, justification, and truth is required in order to answer the "What is knowledge?" question.

If the above analysis is correct, namely, that knowledge requires some mysterious fourth component, then the tripartite analysis fails to adequately capture the concept of knowledge. Perhaps, virtue epistemologists argue, one would believe in the justification of p if one were strong-willed. From here the theory is that epistemic virtues, just like moral virtues, need to be built-up in order for one to acquire knowledge.[9]

But now consider the following possibility: weakness of will is a misnomer. It does not exist, *simpliciter*. But notice that if weakness of will is like a square-circle, a *flatus vocis*, a name given to something that does not truly exist, then the solution to the J question (if one accepts a particular virtue epistemic position) falls apart. The solution tendered to fix the traditional conception of knowledge—namely, that of justified true belief—is no longer viable because there is simply put no such thing as weakness of will.

7. Code, *Epistemic Responsibility.*

8. See Lightbody, *The Problem of Naturalism,* chapter 5.

9. John Greco makes this very argument in his article, "Virtues and Vices of Virtue Epistemology."

For epistemic reasons, it becomes incumbent to question the veracity of weakness of will both in terms of its existence and, if it does exist, whether it is possible to clarify what it involves and when it happens.

It should also be noted that the complexity involved in stating such a question perspicuously, let alone discovering an answer, is not just simply a problem about language. That is to say, the way in which the question of weakness of will is framed is not just a question about semantics as the non-philosopher might put it, for it is the asking and meaning of these questions that serve to underwrite the answers one expects from them. It is what philosophers call a "hard problem." Each question presupposes a unique framework which serves to illuminate the importance of the question. It is the nature of such frameworks that needs to be investigated further.

How is this point not true for all philosophical questions? one might ask. Is it not the case that the question "What is Being?" is, in some sense, already directed because of the way in which the question is asked and indeed in the very asking of the question? And if this the case then what makes the question of weakness of will different from traditional ontological questions regarding Being?

Certainly this objection is not without merit. Heideggerian inclined readers might continue this objection by noting that the question of Being has not been correctly answered in the tomes of the history of philosophy because the question itself, posed as it is in a language that takes a copulative form, distorts any further investigation. And yet while perhaps this point does pack some philosophical punch, there is a sense in which the question along with the questioner desires to get at a foundation or ground, however this might be construed. Of course, Heidegger would call the seeking for a ground "mere metaphysics," but this is beside the point.[10] For though the answer to the question "What is Being?"—such as "substance" or "God"—might be false, there is at least a sense as to what an answer might look like. The question has at least a discernible beginning, even if it has no discernible end.

This is not so with the present question. For the ultimate ground for such a question might very well prove to be eliminable. For example, to substitute *akrasia* (an ancient Greek term that literally means "without power") with "weakness of will" may add some concept that is not necessary to the investigation, namely the notion of will itself. Assuming this

---

10. In *Being and Time*, Martin Heidegger often uses the term "metaphysics," the study of being and of first principles in a pejorative sense.

is the case, "weakness of will," as a translation for *akrasia*, would seem to sneak an ontological extra into the investigation as it were when none might be required. Perhaps an answer to *akrasia* might be forthcoming by understanding the nature of subject and desire, alone. If this is the case, and indeed the early Plato presents a very powerful argument to show how it may be, then introducing an unnecessary concept such as "will" is not only incorrect, but indeed acts as an obstacle to arriving at the true nature of *akrasia*.[11] Thus it is important to tease out the frameworks that make such questions possible and indeed, questionable. The present chapter is dedicated to undertaking this conceptual analysis.

In this chapter, I wish to do two things. Firstly, I will begin my investigation by providing a close analysis of the question "What is *Akrasia*?" Most philosophers, I think it is safe to assume, attempt to provide a conceptual definition of the term they are investigating in order to see whether this definition addresses the two following concerns: (1) "Does this definition adequately explain clear examples of *prima facie* akratic actions?" 2) "Can the definition demonstrate why *prima facie* non-akratic actions are clearly non-akratic?" The goal of this method of philosophy, sometimes referred to as conceptual analysis, is to illuminate linguistic practice and common-sense experience in a non-trivial and interesting manner. But not all uses of conceptual analysis are equally virtuous. Two virtues of well-defined terms are as follows: (1) Can the new definition address counter-examples and seemingly recalcitrant cases in a non-question begging way? 2) Can particularly troublesome counter-examples be reconciled with the definition without the use of ad hoc examples?

My approach, though, will be somewhat different from the one traditionally advanced above. What I do is to begin, simply, with an etymological analysis of the question: "What is *akrasia*?" From this etymological investigation, I uncover a new lens through which to understand both the actions that are usually deemed *akratic* as well as what it means, in general terms, to be an *akratic* individual. This etymological analysis gives way to an emotive or affective analysis. My next task in this chapter is then to take this affective analysis and to detruncate it in order to discover the hidden metaphysical, epistemological, and ethical assumptions under which the question of *akrasia* operates. By exposing these underlying assumptive premises, my hope is to expose a strangely glaring lacunae that exists in the secondary literature, which I call "the void of the *rapport a soi*" (the self's

---

11. See Plato, *Protagoras*.

relationship to itself). I argue that this failure to understand *akrasia* from the perspective of the self's relationship to itself adds a new dimension to solving the problem of *akrasia*.

I use the French term, *rapport a soi,* to identify the meaning that Michel Foucault has given to this term in his series of final volumes dedicated to the care of the self.[12] He claims that modern Western ethical thought has paid very little attention to the "how" of ethics, namely, the methods of self-edification that a self must put into practice in order to realize ethical improvement. Ethicists seem to be more concerned in understanding the *nomoi*: the norms and rules that a subject needs to follow in order to be deemed a good, moral, or virtuous person as the case may be. My analysis, then, is unique in that it consists in unpacking this relationship that a self-identified, weak-willed individual has to herself. This approach provides a further optics through which to view the concept of *akratic* action itself as well as the feeling typically identified as "weak-willed" that invariably follows when one engages in *akratic* behavior, such as when one engages in a clear vice. In addition, my analysis will also shed light on how these feelings affect the relationship a self has to herself.

THE ETYMOLOGY OF *AKRASIA* (ἈΚΡΑΣΙΑ)

I will start by examining the question: "What is *Akrasia*?" *Akrasia* is an ancient Greek word which literally means "without power." It is comprised from the Greek root, *Kratos,* which means power, and "a," which, when placed in front of the root word, means "without" or "no."[13] Such negations are sometimes difficult to capture in English. *Atomos,* for example, is usually defined as indivisible, but a more literal translation is that which cannot be cut. Thus, *akrasia* quite literally means "without power" or "no power."

But what does it mean to be without power? Presumably it would mean that there is a gap between some agenda of an agent and a mode of bringing this agenda to fruition. This seems to be the case when we claim that a person is without power, whether in a household, workplace, or other

12. See the following works for a brief introduction to the notion of the term: Foucault, "What is Enlightenment?" Also see "The Ethic of Care for the Self as a Practice of Freedom" and "An Aesthetics of Existence" also by Foucault. For more on Foucault's "aesthetics of existence" see my previous works: Lightbody, *Philosophical Genealogy Volume 2,* chapter 7.

13. See *The Pocket Oxford Greek-English Dictionary.*

environment. A person in such a situation is unable to put a plan of action into effect. He is unable to assert his own agenda. The individual desires to realize some intention, but can't because there are either external or internal forces at work that prevent him from realizing his ambitions. To be unable to assert one's own agenda, to lack force within an environment, is to no longer be autonomous.

If autonomy is simply the inability to assert one's own agenda, then the next question that follows is simply this: "What prevents the individual from conducting his agenda?" It would appear that we can understand "prevent" in a number of ways. From an external standpoint, prevention might take the form of physical restriction. We might say that the individual, following this model, is quite literally a slave: the person is controlled by some external force or pressure. If one desires to eat and yet cannot get to a fridge because one is chained to a chair, then one is clearly unable to fulfill a very basic desire because of some powerful external force.

I could continue to examine less drastic measures of external prevention, such as legal prevention and so forth, but this would go well beyond the bounds of this book. My primary concern is to look at prevention from an internal standpoint. From my position, I wish to examine autonomy from the inside as it were: from the sense of what is possible for the subject according to the subject's own assessment of himself. Thus, from this internal understanding of autonomy, to be autonomous is to establish a relationship to oneself such that one's intentions have at least some chance of succeeding. Autonomy simply denotes the sense an individual has regarding the degree to which an intention has a chance of succeeding. Certainly our intentions sometimes fail to be realized because of the vicissitudes of circumstance, but this would not undermine the autonomy of an individual as I am using the term. I would argue that autonomy is less about what can in fact be accomplished (as I will show this a pointless intellectual pursuit), but rather the feeling that one is captain of one's fate: one's accomplishments and failures are to some extent the direct result of the free actions of the individual. Another way of putting this is to say that autonomy has more to do with the relationship the individual has established to himself within a given environment (harkening back to Foucault's *rapport a soi*); that is, how freely does one perceive oneself to be?

Thus, to lack power is: (1) to be unable to assert one's agenda in a given context; and, (2) to fail to have a relationship of ownership over oneself.

One has difficulty in actualizing one's intentions, even though there is no external impediment to satisfying said intentions.

An individual is never at zero *vis-a-vis* power: there is always some measure of power that an individual has in any given situation. Following Foucault, even a slave has power insofar as he has the autonomy to submit or not to submit to his master.[14] With that said, lack of power is still tied to the subject's perception of his abilities as well as how these abilities can be used within a given context.

My understanding of a free action (as I am rather loath to define what a free action is, given my approach) differs from that of the traditional definition. The traditional definition holds that in order to be free we must have the ability to act otherwise.[15] My conception does not so much assume this statement to be true, but classifies it as a singularly wrong-headed approach. For even if a scientist had some "determiner device"—an imaginary device that predicted, with 100 percent accuracy, what a person will do in a given situation—this in no way would prove that either the individual or his actions are unfree. Such a machine could only predict what the person would do—but it would not be able to decipher the reasons the individual has for conducting such actions nor the feelings he would receive from committing such actions. And it is these reasons, as well as the feelings that derive from them, that determine our sense of autonomy, or so I am arguing.

Thus autonomy, at least as I am using the concept, denotes a feeling one has to one's environment and to oneself. It is an initial sense of the number and kinds of actions that are freely available to one in a given context, the probable consequences of these actions, and a sense as to what actions one is capable of committing. Thus, to be *akratic* is to be an individual who desires to realize some intention, but can't because he perceives that he does not have the power to put some intention into effect.[16] The "restrictive power" in question could be that the individual cannot deal with the consequences that some action might possibly provoke (as he understands

14. See Foucault's afterword in Dreyfus and Rabinow, *Michel Foucault, Beyond Structuralism and Hermeneutics, Second Edition*.

15. Thomas Hobbes is usually acknowledged as the singular individual to define the commonsense notion of freewill in this rather succinct way (though he did think the idea was incoherent). See his *Of Liberty and Necessity* section 32.

16. There has been much written on the notion of intention in recent years. I do not wish to enter into this debate as it would detract from the main thrust of my argument. With that being said, I take Bratman's view of intention as a mental state that intends to act as a basic starting point. See Bratman, *Intentions, Plans and Practical Reasons*, 3.

them), and although he desires to act in some prescribed manner, does not. Conversely, the individual may feel overcome by some temptation and although he wishes that he could resist it, does not and gives in to this temptation.

In contradistinction, when we claim that an individual has power or great power this phrase denotes that the individual acts in accordance with his intentions. To have power is to feel that (1) one feels one has the capacity to actualize one's intended course of action (there is a sense of ownership of the self; and (2) one initiates these intentions. Given my rendering of autonomy, one is still powerful if one makes an honest attempt to actualize one's intentions. Notice that those who nominally have little freedom, such as prisoners for example, might be *enkratic* or powerful in that they may feel they can take actions, they in fact take these actions as intended, and accept the consequences come what may, even though they were unsuccessful in terms of bringing about the goals of the intended action.

Certainly there are circumstances where it is very difficult to be truly autonomous, but, following Foucault, even here there are still some free manoeuvres that are open to an individual and therefore the flow of power from the agent to his or her circumstances is possible. We might think then that an individual who is said to lack power is an individual who is also controlled, where control connotes influence, coercion, and so forth, but not complete total domination. There are forces that exact a considerable influence over the individual such that the individual in some cases cannot exert his own distinct imprint on the context in question.

This literal definition of the term *akrasia* is helpful in understanding what the Greeks meant by "weakness of will" because the definition of *akrasia* as meaning literally "without power" implies that some thing is lacking control. The akratic individual is not controlled by external forces, however. No, what the *akratic* lacks is *self*-control. The focus of this chapter then is to view *akrasia* through the perspective of control. To be weak-willed is to feel one has little control over one's actions. As we investigate this theme of "without control" in subsequent chapters, it will be shown how Socrates and Plato understand the term and this in turn will help us to understand their respective solutions to the problem: "What is akrasia?"[17]

17. When I speak of Socrates' position on *akrasia* I am referring to the character of Socrates as portrayed in Plato's early dialogues, such as *Protagoras* and *Meno*. When I refer to Plato's position, I am referring to the arguments put forward by Socrates in Plato's middle works such as *Symposium*, *Phaedo* and *Republic*. Vlastos' book, *Platonic Studies*, is very helpful in terms of separating Socrates' thought from that of his student, Plato.

This initial outline of *akrasia* does seem to be at odds with the more traditional understanding of "weakness of will," the most common translation for *akrasia* in the contemporary philosophical literature.[18] Modern renderings of the term seem to define it as acting against one's own best interest. This definition of *akrasia* is clearly delineated by Donald Davidson. In his article, "Weakness of Will," he defines the term as having three conditions. Weakness of will occurs when all three conditions are fulfilled. These conditions are: (1) an agent, Smith, is free to do either X or Y; (2) Smith reasons that X is the best thing to do, all things considered; (3) Smith decides to do Y.[19] One of the seeming advantages of this definition is its appearance of simplicity: *prima facie* it appears that the definition will provide a handy metric for classifying weak-willed actions in an uncomplicated fashion.

Upon further analysis, however, the above definition may appear to be more complex than initially supposed. Consider that the above definition presupposes an understanding of the following terms and phrases: "agency," the rational and normative phraseology "all things considered," "best" (a vague normative qualifier), etc. As noted below, I demonstrate that such terms are not as basic as they appear: we have not reached our goal of hitting bottom by adopting this definition.

To see that such a definition further obfuscates the goal of reaching bottom, consider the following questions that arise when one focuses on the key concepts of Davidson's definition. Firstly, regarding agency, one might ask: "What do we mean by the term 'agent'?" Traditionally, an agent is one who is capable of forming and acting on intentions. The capacity to act on one's intentions is a long-standing definition of autonomy. But if this is correct, then is it possible for a person to display weakness of will in the absence of intention? (E.g., a drug addict.)

Secondly, what do we mean by the phrase "all things considered?" Is it possible to use the same scale to weigh the respective reasons that support two contrary actions? Is it possible to consider a course of action, in light of all things—in terms of a grand narrative? To determine what is best, all things considered, is to assume that one can compare two contrary actions from within the same normative narrative.

---

18. Other translations for *akrasia* are incontinence. See Aristotle's *Nicomachean Ethics Book VII* in this regard.

19. Donald Davidson, "How Is Weakness of the Will Possible?" 22.

If it is possible to weigh the merits of two conflicting choices, all things considered, then one should be able to summon evidence in support for each option and make a rational decision regarding which course of action should be taken. But how does one weigh evidence in this way? Statements become reasons according to a context or framework in which they appear. It is the framework that grants rational authority to a statement. Consider for a moment two normative frameworks: "Be like the country mouse" and Y.O.L.O. (You Only Live Once).[20] Each framework conditions the options that appear within it. A sudden opportunity to go bungee jumping has its reasons for being accepted. Using the framework YOLO, one might reason the following, "In order to live a good life one must complete all the items on one's bucket list and I might not get this opportunity again." But notice that the same opportunity, when viewed from an alternative framework, (be like the country mouse) is no longer deemed choice-worthy. One using such a framework might reason: "Such an activity might be dangerous and it is best not to tempt fate." One does not then choose based on "all things considered," but rather in terms of all things considered *from within framework X.*

Indeed even if one argued that it is possible to view the same choice from two competing frameworks by somehow discovering a common bridge between the two, or alternatively indexing the above two frameworks into a grand narrative, it is still impossible to weigh the two frameworks in an independent manner. That is to say, the goals and underlying assumptions of one framework would irrevocably be reduced to that of the other. The first framework, "Be like the country mouse" suggests that one should first and foremost be prudent and cautious. Why? Because this framework places a premium on security. It assumes that life is long, hard, difficult, and, most significantly, dangerous. Comfort and security are most important. YOLO,

---

20. This is reference to *Aesop's Fables.* In the fable, "The country mouse and the town mouse," a country mouse invites his friend, the town-mouse over to his home. The town mouse is not terribly impressed with the country mouse's dwelling and the limited options before him in terms of food. The town mouse, in an effort of pomposity, invites the country mouse over to his house. The country mouse is at first very impressed with the house and the food the town mouse has to eat. However, there is just one problem: the two mice cannot eat in peace because the house has a cat! Whenever the two are about to eat from the dinner table, the cat is after them, and therefore at best, only a few nibbles of the food on the table can be had before they are running for their lives. The country mouse concludes that it is best to have peace and security over luxury. Marcus Aurelius in book 11 section 21 of his *Meditations,* reminds himself that it is best *to* adopt the country mouse's attitude. See Aurelius, *Meditations,* 112.

however, places value on having profound life experiences and excitement. It reminds us that life is short, tomorrow is never promised, and death is forever. The question then is this: "How does one compare two conflicting frameworks where the goals of each and subsequent reasoning employed to reach said goals, are radically incommensurable?"

Davidson's attempt to provide a conceptual analysis of weakness of will is not without difficulties, as we have seen. But there are problems with Davidson's conceptual analysis method of investigation. A conceptual analysis of a term tries to uncover the real definition of an idea or concept as opposed to the term's lexical definition. Before going any further, it is therefore important to distinguish the two. Lexical definitions are the sort of definitions for words we might find in a dictionary. If I did not know the meaning of the word *inchoate*, for example, I would look up the word and discover that inchoate meant "undeveloped."[21] Real definitions or conceptual definitions are related to lexical definitions since it would be impossible to provide a real definition without having some understanding of how the word one was investigating was used. But real definitions purport to move beyond the lexical definition by identifying the underlying concept that undergirds the word. To present a real definition is to provide the necessary underlying concepts of the idea being investigated, which, when brought together in the proper order, serve to explain the concept sufficiently.[22] For example, if I wished to define justice I might claim that we would need to identify the necessary concepts that serve to explain the word. We might think that one of these words might be fairness as John Rawls held. Justice would then be defined as specific type of fairness.[23]

One of the problems in taking this approach, and it is one that is endemic to the philosophic enterprise as a whole, is best understood by asking: "How do we go about deciding which concepts are in fact contained in others?" To return to the above example, justice as a species of fairness might be thought to be a rather obvious equation for a liberally educated Western individual living in the twenty-first century. But for an ancient Greek it is quite clear that justice could never be equated with fairness. For the ancient Greek male who was of noble birth, justice simply denotes dispensing just desserts. As MacIntyre notes in his seminal work, *Whose*

---

21. See Rauhut's helpful discussion regarding the difference between these two terms in Rauhut, *Ultimate Questions*, 21.

22. Ibid., 21–22.

23. See Rawls, "Justice as Fairness: Political Not Metaphysical."

Justice? Which Rationality: "To be wronged is to be the recipient of unde-served harm inflicted intentionally by someone else. To redress wrong is to restore the order in which the appropriate goods, whatever they are, are distributed according to dessert."[24] Whose conception of justice is correct? The idea of justice, one might then infer, is contingent upon the social, eco-nomic, and historical setting of the individual for whom justice is applied along with to whom justice is applicable. A conceptual analysis of justice then, from this perspective, is a false starter.

Such difficulties would seemingly apply to *akrasia*. After all, if it is reasonable to believe that justice, as an idea, is one that is woven by many weavers using many threads, then *ceteris paribus, akrasia,* as an idea that simply connotes lack of power, would be subject to these same vicissitudes. One could perhaps argue, *pace* the genealogist, that the litmus to determine which concept (justice or *akrasia*) is more primordial is determined by the depth and purity of feeling that each concept elicits.[25]

Both notions, though, seem to elicit some very powerful emotive reac-tions in those who, for example, have suffered acts of injustice and for those who engage in akratic actions. Such affective responses, while very differ-ent, can be equally powerful. For example, a person passed up for a promo-tion in favor of someone with less experience, less talent, may certainly feel that he has been treated in an unjust manner. And this feeling that some injustice has been committed may be felt rather acutely and for a prolonged period of time. But likewise the individual who is weak-willed may also ex-perience profound regret over some action that he or she has self-evaluated as stemming from weakness or perhaps a powerful temptation. Depth and purity of emotion, it would seem, are not enough to determine which of the two concepts is more primal.

There might be another way to justify a genealogical or emotive ap-proach to understanding an idea. The genealogist argues that the basic engine behind all human action is that of power or more perspicuously, a desire to express one's power. The argument, then, is that if we could but

---

24. MacIntyre, *Whose Justice? Which Rationality?* 33.

25. Philosophical genealogy is a method of historical inquiry first developed by Friedrich Nietzsche. He argued that all ideas evolve from those of others, sometimes their opposite and therefore no idea is self-contained. Moreover, ideas whether philo-sophical, theological, or moral are often rationalizations of more primitive irrational desires. What's more, one could determine the pedigree and ancestry of a concept by tracing its emotive elements. For a full account of genealogy see Lightbody, *Philosophical Genealogy.*

reduce the feeling of injustice and the feeling of being weak-willed to a more basic common denominator then the method of affective analysis would remain intact. It would still be possible to reach bottom—the goal of the present book.

An act of injustice is not simply the breaking of a moral code, but is an action that hurts or is perceived to hurt some person. An individual passed over for a job has been hurt financially, emotionally, socially. But just as important, there is a sense in which the individual does not have control over the course of his life. Some other individual is able "to pull the levers" as it were, and despite the person's best efforts he can never advance in the company. This might very well be the greatest sting of injustice, namely, the feeling that one is powerless. But likewise, an individual who is weak-willed has also been "hurt" (ashamed) in that he did not act on what he perceived his best interest to be. The individual is incapable of pursuing what is in his best interest and therefore feels powerless in the face of his desires. He is unable to rein in these desires and therefore suffers as a result. Again, with weakness of will, it is this feeling of powerlessness that stings us so greatly. Thus, the basic optic through which I will investigate the phenomenon of weakness of will, namely, as a feeling of powerlessness, here construed as lack of control, remains a valid starting point. Indeed, it seems to be a basic starting point for other philosophical investigations (e.g., an affective analysis of injustice).

My task is to follow this line of inquiry, namely, the feelings associated with what we cognitively perceive to be weakness of will and how these feelings stem from a perceived lack of control. Despite the difficulties mentioned above, we may continue to analyze the question: "What is *Akrasia*?" along four lines of thought. Firstly, what exactly is this *thing* that is lacking control? Is it a self? a person? an agent? or what?

Secondly, how is this entity comprised? Does it consist of parts, and, if so, what are the natures of such parts? How do these parts interact with other parts of this thing to form a whole? Are these parts unified by some higher principle? And if so, what established this unity and what continues to unify the whole?

Thirdly, what does it mean to say that it, whatever this "it" may be, is *without* control? More precisely, how should we interpret the qualifier "without"? Are we to interpret control in some sense that might be essential to the thing in question such that the very thing is defined by this notion of control as its essence? Or is control best understood as that of a sovereign's rule: more like a law-like order that applies across the board to all phenomena?

Fourthly, what *is* this sort of control, rule, or power that this thing lacks? What is the ultimate source of control? From where does it derive its power? Can control be interpreted in a legal sense where transgression is possible, but frowned upon? The rest of this chapter will attempt to answer the above questions.

QUESTION THREE:
WHAT DOES IT MEAN TO SAY THAT IT, WHATEVER THIS "IT" MAY BE, IS WITHOUT CONTROL?

I want to start with the third question. To claim that something is without control or rule is to claim that such a thing is without order or law. But even here we can proceed to make further clarifications. Things may be ordered and law-like, but it would be strange to call such things "self-ruled." A number series may be ordered such that we know what the next number in the series will be. If we have a number series like 2 . . . 4 . . . 6 . . . 8 we might claim that the function of the series is N+2. However it would be a terribly strange state of affairs to describe the numbered series as "self-ruled." When we employ the term "self-ruled" or describe an individual as *enkratic* we mean to say that an agent has control of his or her actions. The agent is his own ruler and, as a ruler, is able to implement intentions and plans of action effortlessly.

Let us take a less abstract and more concrete example. Take the Law of the Conservation of Mass. The Conservation of Mass states that an isolated system will remain constant with respect to its molecular mass over time. Such a concept is important in explaining the simple phenomenon of understanding why wood loses mass when it is burned. The carbon from the wood reacts with the oxygen in the air causing the wood to lose carbon molecules. However, the total mass of the wood is never truly lost. The mass is simply transferred from the wood to the air. If the wood was just as heavy post-burning as the wood prior to being burned, then we might say that the wood did not behave according to the physical law. It is inexplicably not under the control of this law.

But again it would be strange to call this system "self-ruled" in the way in which we think of a person as self-ruled. The system obeys (or disobeys) a law of nature, but obey in this sense of the word is used anthropomorphically. It would appear then that en*kratic or continent* at least minimally entails that one is aware of the rule that one follows. At a minimum, *conscious* and *wilful* obeyance of a rule would seem to be a necessary condition for self-rule.

Following Aristotle, I would suggest that it is incumbent to make a distinction between the temperate man and the continent man. In the former case, the temperate individual is born to be in control of his desires. He is never out of balance, as it were, and therefore neither consciously nor willfully is *enkratic*. This is not so for the continent man. The continent individual is tempted, but the relationship he has to himself is one where his potential to engage in vice is never actualized: he lives up to his virtuous character precisely because he does not act on his temptations. Despite feeling misaligned at times (the continent man's best intentions do not line up with his desires), the continent man remains continent: he does not follow through on his temptations. He consciously and deliberately chooses not to fulfill certain desires.[26]

The above discussion brings to light an interesting question: If the conscious, willful, and successful obeyance of some normative rule of behavior is a necessary condition for strength of will, is it also a sufficient condition? Consider a thought experiment that examines self-rule from the perspective of strength of will. The traditional interpretation of weakness of will holds that if an individual acts against his best interest and yet is free to act on this interest, then he is weak-willed. Thus a person is continent, to use Donald Davidson's definition of continence, if he always acts according to his best interests, all things considered (or his most well-thought-out reasons or his best intentions or any other normative qualifier one might wish to substitute).[27] If this is the case, though, then what is the answer to the following question: Would the above agent, continent though he may be, be *enkratic*? Notice this is different from claiming that he is continent in the Davidsonian sense of the term. (For simplicity I shall call Davidson's idea of continence D-continence).

D-continence simply suggests that the individual always acts in conformance with his best interests. But this is not the same as saying that the individual has power or control over his desires. One might be D-continent by sheer accident: one is simply a temperate, sensible individual who is not prone to rash actions. It is for this reason that Aristotle, for example,

26. See Aristotle, *Nichomachean Ethics, Book VII.*
27. Davidson, "How Is Weakness of the Will Possible?" 41.

would reject the juxtaposition that Davidson sets up *vis-a-vis* continent and weak-willed individuals. For at this juncture there is no discernible difference between the man of temperance and the continent individual, at least according to Aristotle. For Aristotle, the temperate man's actions are the same as those of the continent individual's, but it is the *intention* that differs. The temperate man cannot help but be temperate: he is so built, that, try as he might, he has no wish to engage in vice. This is not the case for the continent individual. Thus, acting in accordance with one's perceived best interests is certainly not a sufficient condition to determine *enkratia* or strength of will.

The above discussion leads us to an important question regarding Davidson's notion of continence: "Would one claim that an agent who is deemed D-continent (i.e., one who always followed his best interest at all times) lived a life that, when viewed as a whole, *really* followed his own best interests?" According to some thinkers, like George Ainslie, the answer to this question would be a definite no. An individual who always followed his own best interests would, on the whole, not lead a life where his best interests were always followed and, therefore, to pursue one's best interests in a controlled, rationally determined fashion is to fail to achieve them.[28]

This idea, namely that to exercise D-continence always and in all circumstances is to fail to achieve it over the course of one's life, might seem strange at first glance, but consider one aspect that surely makes life worth living: spontaneity. Surely, Ainslie suggests, spontaneity is one of those necessary properties for a well-lived life. It provides the *je ne sais quoi* coloring to one's lived experience. By definition, spontaneous actions cannot be planned; they cannot be part of the weighing of all things considered, and yet some actions that are undertaken spontaneously resonate with individuals and become, in time, important and indeed life-defining experiences.

From the above reflections, it is clearly questionable as to whether such a human agent, dedicated to calculating his best interests at every juncture in his life, could exist. Such an agent who always acted according to his best considered reasons may not lack control in the strict sense of incontinence, at least as traditionally defined, but is surely not in control of his life either. The agent is so determined to maintain whatever course of action he has deemed to be best or most reasonable at whatever the cost that an alternative is never tried, let alone conceived. There is, in other words, no real sign of domination, no sense of overpowering, and therefore the agent is not

28. Ainslie, *Breakdown of Will*, chapter 9: "The Down Fall of Willpower."

enkratic: power is not wielded by the agent, but by some alien, innate force. In this example, the agent would resemble more of an automaton than a person.

In order for an agent to be *enkratic,* to have power, control, there must be some counter-force, some form of resistance. Even Odysseus, who is often thought of as the Greek paradigm for endurance, right-mindedness, determinateness, etc., was tempted by the Sirens, as one might recall. Indeed it is for this very reason that he had his men bind him to the mast of the ship beforehand—he desired to hear the Siren's call and knew that if unrestrained he would give up his most cherished ideal: saving his kingdom and reuniting with Penelope.[29] Conscious rule—where one recognizes that there are real possibilities before one that would not be in one's best interest—would seem to be a necessary requirement for *enkratia.* Unconscious rule would not be ruling at all.

QUESTION ONE:
WHAT IS THIS SELF THAT IS RULED?

How then should we interpret conscious rule or power over the self? What kind of power are we discussing? Moreover, what does it mean to say that one consciously rules the self? What is one ruling over? This line of questioning would seem to presuppose at least two elements: the object being ruled and the entity responsible for such ruling. Both elements, of course, refer to the same entity: the self. But what is the self? We are now in a position to explore question one: "What does it mean to say that the self is ruled?" "What is the self so ruled?"

To be sure, it is possible and indeed desirable for the purposes of investigating whether *akrasia* can be overcome for both of the above relations to belong to the one and same ontological thing. For if it were the case that the entity we call the self along with all its properties of conscious reflection, memory, mood, desires, beliefs, intentions, and so forth, is ultimately ruled by something outside of itself then the study of *akrasia* would be for nought: by definition we could not form a relationship to some entity that, as matter of course, cannot be related to the self. This idea of forming a relationship with one's self seems to be a key component to self-development.

Søren Kierkegaard expressed this notion of the self as a relationship to itself rather tersely when he wrote: "The self is a relation which relates

29. Homer, *The Odyssey.*

itself to its own self or it is the relation that the relation relates itself to its own self."[30] Kierkegaard will go on to adumbrate the kinds of existential relations the self might form to itself. I will not discuss these here. But I will take up this basic understanding of the self, that is as a self-reflexive relation, and apply it to the problem of *akrasia*.

Of course, there are many other ways to conceive of the relationship that the self has to itself. These different conceptions of the self will also entail different relations that one may have to oneself. Certainly there is a line of interpretation held by both the "middle Plato" and Aristotle that would support the idea that what some might call the self—soul or psyche, and what Descartes would call the mind—must work in conjunction with the body.[31] Both the middle Plato and Aristotle would hold that there are non-rational desires within the same self. Such desires are non-rational in the sense that reason cannot completely prevent us from having them and indeed they seemingly appear to run counter to the goals of reason itself. For Plato and Aristotle, the goal of reason, very crudely put here, is to gain more knowledge, because only knowledge will lead to a flourishing life. Whether such a flourishing life is defined as *Eudaimonia* (Aristotle) or is defined as the lover of wisdom (Plato) matters little. Reason for both Plato and Aristotle, to quote Socrates in *Protagoras,* is the most powerful thing we possess and can assist us in understanding and controlling non-rational desires.[32] But make no mistake, such desires will continue to emanate quite independently on their own.

If Plato and Aristotle are correct, then we might conclude, again minimally, that the self must relate to itself in accordance with reason in order to be truly happy. Of course, the question then is: "What is reason?" The ancient Greek philosophers, such as Plato (or at least the early Plato), Epicurus, Epictetus, and others, seem to have a very robust view of reason: the idea is to allow reason full rule of the self. Reason should rule over our passions, actions, and desires. But this is not the only way to understand the relationship that reason should have to a subject or agent. For example, it is consistent to say that, yes, one must rule one self with reason in mind, but one must also recognize that reason itself is only a tool for desire and that it is desire that is the true engine for action.

30. Kierkegaard, *The Sickness unto Death,* 146.

31. When I refer to the middle Plato, I am referring to Plato's middle dialogues (those written when Plato was middle aged) such as *Phaedo, Symposium,* and *Republic.*

32. See Plato, *Protagoras,* 352c–d, 782.

The above position (where reason is but a tool for desire) is clearly articulated and vigorously defended by David Hume. Hume argued that reason is no more than an instrument: it is a mere instrument for desire. Reason, Hume evinces, "is and ought to be the slave of the passions and can never pretend to any other office than to serve and obey them."[33] Desires are the true push-pull engines of the soul. In more contemporary terminology, I would think that reason is much like a computer program that generates a schema that allows a subject to realize his or her desires by simply putting plans into effect to achieve them. Any moral position which asserts otherwise runs counter to human nature, or so argues Hume.

Despite holding a seemingly contrary view of reason to that of Plato and Aristotle, Hume must still give reason a significant place in his moral schema. For Hume, a subject needs to employ reason in order to satisfy his or her more deeply held desires. If one desires to lose weight in order to look better in his or her new jeans, for example, then this desire will run counter to other desires and/or hypothetical maxims. For example, a subject (call her Pam) desperately wants to fit into an old pair of jeans but also has a sweet tooth, and as such has adopted the following hypothetical maxim: "I should always eat dessert if it is offered to me."[34] Pam's always eating dessert conflicts with her desire to lose weight.[35]

If it is possible and indeed very likely that two desires will often run counter to each other then which desire wins out? Who acts as the referee in such matters? Hume's answer: reason!

Yet reason, even for the Humean, still does the same job as it does for Plato and Aristotle. Even if we pare down reason to "best considered judgment to achieve some end" or "doing what is in one's best interest" or

33. Hume, *A Treatise of Human Nature,* 415. Of course, Hume also argued that we were capable of feeling empathy for others. To feel empathy for another is a causal condition where we are suddenly placed in the shoes of the other as it were.

34. I am borrowing the term hypothetical maxim from Kant. Kant makes a distinction between hypothetical maxims on the one hand and moral maxims on the other. Maxims for all intents and purposes are simply plans of action—they prescribe what one should to do in a given circumstance. Hypothetical maxims are not *prima facie* moral, e.g., I should always tie an untied shoelace. Moral maxims are universal and hold true for all of humanity. They are informed and grounded by the categorical imperative. See Kant, *Groundwork for the Metaphysics of Morals.*

35. We might employ Frankfurt's terminology of first- and second-order desires to help explain that not all internal conflict involves the combatants of reason and desire. My project in some ways overlaps with Frankfurt's position. See Frankfurt, "Freedom of the Will and The Concept of a Person," 5–20.

any other rational schema that attempts to maximize the return on those things that we most desire, reason remains responsible for reining in some activity which is somehow foreign to it. Let us return to Pam's dilemma: in determining whether to have the dessert presented before her, she must weigh the immediate pleasure she would receive from eating the dessert against the guilt she might feel for giving up on her resolution to fit into an old pair of jeans. If she holds onto her initial goal of fitting into her jeans then she has certainly reined in what is perhaps a very strong desire to eat a cupcake, for example. Thus, even if one is a Humean, the problem of *akrasia* remains: What rules? For to rein in some appetite that is somehow different and contrary from what you identify as your true desire and yet in some very real sense emanates from you, is to recognize a contrary agenda to what you identify (depending on the position) as a second order desire or a desire that once achieved represents some goal that you identify with as belonging to your "true" self. It is to recognize that there is something else, within you, that has its own engine as it were and is driven to pursue its own end, contrary to your own plans. Reason, even if minimally construed as some calculator for maximizing desires, still comes to provide an answer. But, unlike a calculator, the answer is not necessarily deemed "correct" for we may always reassess the calculation. Pam, for example, may reason: "While it is true that I do desire to fit into my old jeans, having one cupcake is not going to make a difference in achieving this goal. Therefore, I should have the cupcake." *Akrasia* cannot seemingly be explained using a simple Humean calculus because surely we would explain Pam's behavior by exclaiming that a different calculator has been employed! She is being weak-willed.[36]

Thus, reason must be something more than a mere calculator for when it is said that we rein in something as reason sometimes does (sometimes it doesn't though!) this would seem to imply that such a strong desire may conflict with the agenda we initially set for the self and yet reason has some power over this other desire. If we accept the Humean picture for a moment, it is often the case that reason is brought in as reinforcement, as it were, to buttress an initially weak desire. When we are truly pulled by two contrary desires, it is the stronger of the two that will win, unless reason comes to the aid of the weaker desire. Thus it is possible for an initially weak desire

36. According to Thomas E. Hill Jr., Hume's account of willpower is such that it, willpower, is not causally efficacious: it is neither a strong nor weak power in Hume's terminology and therefore weakness of will does not exist. See Hill, "Kant on Weakness of Will," 215.

to win out over a much stronger desire—this circumstance however would not be possible if it were not for reason. Indeed, the very notion of "reining something in" presupposes that some measure of strength is required to control the engine of this other power.

If the above discussion has some credence to it, then it is clear that we, as subjects, are simply desiring machines, whatever else we may be.[37] Desires will always be present within us, but it is possible to dampen the force of these desires. Indeed, as Plato will show, it is even possible to transform base desires into skyhooks for rationality.

QUESTION 2:
WHAT IS THE NATURE OF THIS RULE
AND WHAT EXACTLY IS BEING RULED?

This question of reining in something which has its own agenda provides us with a new angle from which to understand the question: "What rules?" It would appear that to rule over something is to have power over it in some way. And conversely to be without rule is to lack power. Examining the first statement, we might say that the question of rule is a question of power. Thus, to speak about *akratic* actions is to speak about the self as having no control or no power. Certainly this understanding would hold true for both the middle Plato (the Plato of the *Republic)* and Aristotle: to be ruled by desire entirely is to be a slave of desire completely. Aristotle would certainly argue that the self-indulgent man is a clear example of this kind of desire-slavery, whereas, for Plato, the paradigm of desire-slavery would clearly be the tyrannical individual.[38] Even if we accept Hume's account, namely, that desire alone is responsible for driving us to act, a distinction between first-order and second-order desires must be maintained. For to be controlled by first-order desires such that these pursuits get in the way of attaining our second-order desires, our "true" or "authentic" desires, then even our own most cherished subjective plans of action will fail. We will be slaves to our first-order desires. Thus, whether we hold a desiring account of subjectivity where reason is minimally construed or a more robust rational account, the question still needs to be asked: "In what sense does the self lack power?" It

37. See Deleuze and Guatarri, *Anti-Oedipus, Capitalism and Schizophrenia.*

38. See Aristotle, *Nicomachean Ethics,* Book VII section 8. See Plato, *Republic,* Book IX 571e, 1180.

would appear that we need now to investigate what is meant by power, rule and what is in fact ruled.

To answer what is meant by "power" and specifically the special kind of power that is discussed when one mentions will-power or self-control, it might be helpful to begin with a modern understanding of power from the perspective of physics. Power, in this framework, is defined as the rate in which energy is transferred from one thing to another. One way to understand this is to think of electrical power. The amount of light a lightbulb can produce is known *via* its wattage. The higher the wattage, the more energy the lightbulb can transfer over time. More germane to our discussion, however, is the definition of power in terms of work. Work is defined as the force an object exerts on another. Work in a mechanical sense is defined as the distance the object moves over time. This notion of power is more amenable for our purposes. So power, when taken in this sense, is just the capacity to do work.

I once read a car report which stated that it felt like the car had "a lot of power on tap." What I understood from this description is that the car can reach highway speeds with only slight pressure on the accelerator. There is a definite sense that if we "floored it" the car would accelerate at a breathtaking pace. The car has the capacity for much a greater expression of its horsepower. Horsepower is, of course, a unit of measurement for work. The term horsepower was originally used to explain how many horses would be required to equal the output of a steam engine. Steam engines at first were used, primarily, to draw water from mines.[39] Thus, "horsepower" as a unit was used to define how many horses would be required (taking into consideration the horses' need for rest, etc.) to draw water from a mine such that the mine would remain operable. I want to explore this relation between "lacking power" in the practical wisdom sense and the notion of "lacking power" in this mechanical sense to see if we can continue to extrapolate an insight from this analogy. Is it possible to outline some common ground between the two and if we can, will this provide us with a new lens through which to view power along with relationship between the self to itself?

From this all too brief analysis there is a sense in which to be without power is to be unable to perform some sort of work. To be able to do work implies several more components—both ontological and epistemological. To work is to work on some thing. The thing in question, usually, is some

39 See the article in the Encyclopedia Britannica entitled "horsepower" http://www.britannica.com/EBchecked/topic/272384/horsepower

sort of object external to oneself, such as when someone states: "I intend to work on the car tonight." But work can be performed on the self. If one is prone to say things before thinking them through one might say: "I intend to work on that aspect about myself, in the future I will be more circumspect." In any case, work seems to imply a very special relationship between an agent and an object. This relationship implies that there is an intention on the part of an agent to improve the agent's relation to the object. In the case of working on one's car, the agent might decide to improve the car for a host of reasons: he needs to fix the car because he needs it to get to work, he is unhappy with how the car looks, etc. To improve the relationship one has to an object, at this stage of the investigation, is relative to the agent's notion of what such an improvement might entail. The point of the analogy is to see whether we can illuminate the relationship between work, power, or the lack thereof, and *akrasia*.

Continuing with this line of thinking we might claim that to rein in some thing is to undermine its power to reach some goal. But why do we rein in such a desire? Given the above understanding, we rein in such a desire because it interferes with our work. For example, take the process of losing weight. As anyone who has tried to lose weight knows, this process is extremely difficult. An individual clearly has a desire to lose weight and yet has other, contrary desires such as eating sugary or high-fat snacks. Or again, if an individual, let's call him Bob, has established that he only has time and energy to go for a jog immediately after work at time t and, that such a habit, if practiced consistently, will help Bob reach his desired goal weight, then any other desire at time t that conflicts with the act of jogging will undermine the fulfillment of the goal. It is clear that there may be conflicts between two or more competing desires. If the desire to watch television wins out over the desire to jog at time t, then clearly this new desire (e.g., watching television) runs counter to the overall goal, namely, that of weight loss.

By thinking about the question of power in this way, namely, in thinking about desires *simpliciter* as forces that push and pull in precise directions, we venture onto the borders of the fourth question: "What does it mean to say that something is without *rule?*" "What precisely is this *rule?*" There are different ways to undermine the power of something, after all. One can, of course, simply overpower something else. In this sense to rein something else in, to rule it, is to prevent the latter thing from pursuing its goal by matching the propulsion of the latter thing with an equal or greater measure of force. One clear example of this might be described as simply "willing" not to commit some action. Reining in a desire in this case would be like pulling back a dog on a leashed-collar from some object or person. The owner, if strong enough, can simply redirect the dog by overpowering it. When we choose not to engage in some self-destructive behavior that has dire consequences, by "pulling on the leash of the desire" just like the dog-owner above, we feel that a battle has been won. We have overcome some enemy that perhaps at this moment in time was not equal to our resolve, but certainly is something to be reckoned with.

Still another way of reining some entity in is to apply pressure on some sensitive part of such a thing: such as when a horseback rider pulls on the reins of the horse thereby applying pressure on the tongue of the horse via the bridle and bit and thereby forcing the horse to stop. In a sense, this practice saps the propulsion of the force in a less direct, but in many other ways, more effective manner than the dog and leash example above. For this manner of "desire-reining" presupposes an intimate knowledge of the desire in question. One way of perfecting this kind of technique is to understand the desire on a meta-cognitive level. Jon Elster discusses such meta-cognitions of desire in his profound and comprehensive work, *Alchemies of the Mind*.

In the work, Elster is at pains to show that all desiring is infused with cognition. He argues that by understanding the evolution of a particular deleterious desire, that is, how a desire is transformed *via* reflection, that one can then form techniques by which to negate the effects of the desire. Negating the effects of some desire is very often a natural process of many human beings, especially if two conditions are present: (1) the desire is not something that can be easily quenched; and (2) the object of desire is something that is satisfied by others in one's social circle. When these conditions are present, it is not simply the case that the agent feels hurt because some desire cannot be satisfied. Instead he might feel a plethora of meta-emotions, such as shame, guilt, etc., that will have a greater impact on his self-esteem because others are able to satisfy the desire when he proves incapable. According to Elster, we are so built to abstain from feeling cognitive dissonance that we will do almost anything to re-write the script of what we are seeing.[40] For example, let's assume that it is John's most heartfelt desire to own a Ferrari. John is also aware that his neighbor, Mike, also desires to own a Ferrari and both Mike and John have had many

40. Elster, *Alchemies of the Mind*, 42–43.

conversations in which each discussed how happy owning such a vehicle would make them. John does not make any sacrifices to turn this dream into reality. He squanders his money, makes unwise financial investments, gambles, etc. Mike, though, through saving and careful investing is able to afford a Ferrari after a number of years and drives up John's driveway to show John. John is first overcome with what Elster would call a basic feeling of envy and thinks, "Mike has something I want, something I yearn for." But then, John experiences a meta-cognition: he feels ashamed for he too realizes that if he were more careful then he too would have been able to afford a Ferrari. However, because we as humans are so built to avoid cognitive dissonance, where we experience negative, hurtful feelings which may disrupt how we view ourselves and the world, we represses this cognition, namely, "if I were more careful I could have had what my neighbor has." Instead, John believes, incorrectly, that Mike was able to afford the Ferrari through some illicit means—he inherited the money to purchase the car from his rich uncle whom he duped, or he cheated on his taxes, etc. And from reflecting on these possibilities, John's basic emotion of envy changes to that of indignation. This feeling might even be more charged than John's initial feeling of envy, but it is a feeling that is more palatable and certainly one that is less hurtful than the emotion of shame, which if felt for a prolonged period of time may disrupt other attitudes he has about himself, e.g., he is not a spendthrift, he does not make poor financial decisions, etc.

Cognizing desires on a meta-level can be very helpful *vis-a-vis* resisting some temptation. According to Elster, such desires may be transmuted into positive energy by a simple process of reflection. For example, look at the case of Greg. Greg desires to lose weight, but finds the process difficult because of his wife, Sue. Sue is prone to buying snacks and other treats that Greg loves even though Greg has asked Sue to not buy such treats because Greg cannot exercise restraint when he eats them. Greg has committed himself to losing weight and has been doing well for the past week. Greg looks into his fridge after working out to eat some carrot sticks when he sees his favorite cake dead-center of the fridge. The cake has a note on it from Sue which reads, "Just a little reward for all your hard-work losing weight." Greg is at first angry: he is angry at Sue for buying the cake and for the note left on it. Nevertheless, he is very hungry and has a strong desire to eat the cake. But, as he reflects on the note, he becomes enraged and ends up throwing the cake in the garbage. Greg's strong desire to eat the cake has been turned into righteous indignation: a desire to show his wife that he is "in charge." The desire to eat has been transmuted into a desire for revenge.

Still another way to prevent some entity from arriving at its true goal is to divert its energy towards something else. Plato, in the work *Phaedrus,* seems to advocate this strategy. According to Plato, the self is like a horse-drawn chariot. The entire vehicle consists of two horses and a charioteer. One horse is white and represents the noble virtues. The second is dark and symbolizes the appetites of the soul that are most closely associated with the body (e.g., material wealth, sex, food, etc.). Finally, the charioteer represents reason. Plato argues that in order to remove inner conflict we should not attempt to extirpate such dark passions.[41] Instead we should try to harness them: in order for the charioteer to reach his goal, which is that of virtue *via* reason, he needs to harness the nascent desire for all things bodily and replace this desire for a goal on a spiritual order. The desire to accumulate material things may be transformed into a desire to accumulate knowledge. Freud of course picked up on this idea and formed his own tripartite analysis of soul in the form of the Ego, Id, and Super-Ego.[42]

Another strategy is to allow the desire some fulfillment, but never complete satisfaction. This strategy allows the desire to quench some of its thirst, but only to a certain extent. In this case, we do not extinguish desire, but corral it: we are providing the desire with some room of movement within a boundary prescribed beforehand by reason. To continue with the example given above regarding weight loss, low calorie desserts would be an example of corralling what might be a particularly destructive desire. The desire to eat sweet treats is pacified with a substitute product: perhaps the dessert is made with aspartame or sucralose, etc. The food may not be an exact replacement, but it is a substitute and suffices at least, for now. The individual who uses such techniques to curb a potentially destructive desire has seemingly reached a compromise: there is recognition that the full thrust behind the desire cannot be extinguished but merely tempered.

The above list is by no means meant to be exhaustive and I do not mean to provide a peculiar taxonomy of the different ways in which one might rule over some desire that runs counter to the sort of deep meaningful work one has set for oneself. However, I would be remiss if I did not at

---

41. Plato instead counsels that we should learn to become our "best friend." This -notion of becoming our best friend will be further explored in chapters 3 and 4. See Plato, *Phaedrus,* 506–57.

42. See Freud, *Beyond the Pleasure Principle.*

least mention one other way to rule over a particularly harmful desire. That way is what we might call extirpation. To extirpate a desire is to remove it completely and in most cases would seem to presuppose that the individual has become a completely different person.

My father is an example of an individual who successfully extirpated a particularly lengthy desire to smoke. Prior to suffering from a heart attack at the age of sixty-two, my father had been a smoker for well over forty years. My father would come home from work and without fail, light up a cigarette and watch TV. This would be followed by another cigarette or two just before dinner. After dinner, my father would have at least another two or three before going to bed. All told, my father smoked at least twenty-five cigarettes a day for forty years. To his credit my father was able to break his dependency on nicotine nearly immediately after having triple bypass surgery and never smoked another cigarette (or at least there was no evidence of smoking as far I could tell) for the rest of his life, some thirteen years after his first heart attack.

I once asked my father, "Why did you give up smoking? How were you able to quit cold turkey?" As my father explained it, his revelation or epiphany came when, a few days after his surgery, he went to the smoker's waiting room in the hospital with the intention of having a cigarette. But upon taking one breath of that foul, smoked-filled air all desire to smoke left him. About a year after he quit smoking I asked him, "Do you still have the urge to smoke? Do you ever have the desire to light one up?" And he turned around and said to me, "After that day in the waiting-room, all desire to smoke was simply gone." The extirpation of the desire to smoke was a rather passive affair: my father had every intention to smoke when he entered into that room, but fate or physiology as the case may be, intervened. We might call this sort of extirpation passive extirpation: the desire simply disappears as a direct and immediate unexpected result because of some event or situation.

Active extirpation is another kind of "desire-removal process." This type of extirpation is best exemplified by Christian apologists such as Evagrius. Evagrius was an early Christian ascetic. He argued that in order not to commit one of the seven deadly sins one could use the sins against each other. The most powerful emotion one could employ to fight off sinful behavior, at least according to Evagrius, was pride. For example, assume John is very hungry and he desires to attend an all-you-can-eat-buffet. John knows it is very likely that he will over-indulge and eat too much. If he does, he will commit the sin of gluttony. One possible way of fighting glut-tony might be to abstain from attending the buffet—but this is not what Evagrius counsels. For even indulging in the thought of food, entertaining the pleasure that one might receive from feeling "stuffed" or from tasting many different dishes, is already to sin, or so Evagrius argues. He argues that if John reflected on how gluttonous behavior destroyed his self-esteem, his vanity, with each time he walks up to the buffet, then John might very well go up only once. Thus, in order to prevent lustful thoughts of food or indulge in outright corpulent behavior, John would do well to appeal to his vanity—he might reflect on what is going on around him and think, "Look at all these individuals indulging in their basic appetites—I am stronger than they are because I can keep my appetites in check."

Of course, indulging in such thoughts would entail that John was committing the sin of vanity, but this too, Evagrius counsels, could also be checked. John might remind himself that he only refrains from engaging in such gluttonous actions because his spirits are buoyed by God. Or he might think, "Although I am able to resist such foods, I am tempted by them and therefore I should remain humble." For Evagrius, it is not enough to refrain from acting on some impulse; the real test is to extirpate, immediately, the impulse from the mind before one can contemplate it, for to contemplate the indulgence of some desire is just as immoral as engaging in it.

The goal for Evagrius was to reach a state of *apathia* or apathos, where one would no longer be pushed or pulled by sinful behavior. Obviously such reflective, self-conscious expunging of desires by means of obsessively checking and re-checking what one was feeling, would, I am sure, have been a very tortuous affair.[43] Certainly it is not one that I counsel here in this book, but it is important to mention in order to show that contrary powerful and corpulent desires may be used, transformed, and indeed transmuted by reason for higher, spiritual purposes.

I would argue that there is no hard and fast line between passive and active extirpation. Certainly, in my father's case, the work in a sense was done for him—one event caused the desire to smoke to be removed com-pletely. Evagrius marks an extreme case in that active extirpation would be an activity that would have needed to be employed on a minute by minute basis. I think most individuals fall somewhere in between: certainly extirpa-tion has been practiced by Christian mystics and many others, but I would think that there is a middle ground: the individual has been transformed in

43. Sorabji, *Emotions and Peace of Mind*, 360–61.

some profound way and therefore the force of specific desires—think of the seven deadly sins—has been significantly blunted. There is still work for the individual to perform, but the work is not as strenuous as the work seemingly performed by Evagrius. I will examine this middle way in more detail when I turn to Plato's solution to the problem of *akrasia* in chapter three.

In summary, to rule the self, or more appropriately to rule over desires such that they do not rule us, cannot be answered in a "one-size fits all" manner. One may try to extirpate all desires, but this approach, over the long-run, will be unsuccessful. One may also corral them, transmute them or employ mixed strategies with varying degrees of success (e.g., one may choose to extirpate some harmful desires [when viewed from a second-order level] and corral most of the others). Plato's approach (transmutation) will be the one argued for here in the present work.

QUESTION 4:
WHAT DOES IT MEAN TO LACK
OR TO BE WITHOUT POWER?

We are now able to turn to the fourth question proper: "What does it mean to *lack* power?" What does it mean to be *without* rule? Given the above interpretation, to lack power or to be *akratic* then, is to be incapacitated. But it is to be incapacitated in a very special sense of the term: it is to be incapable of performing some type of work. What is this work? Simply the capacity to improve the relationship one has to oneself. The notion of failing to improve one's relationship to oneself, at this point, can be viewed from two perspectives: (1) There is an intention to work on some object, in this case the self, but there is a gap between the intention and performance of the action. More specifically, the *Akrates* or weak-willed individual is unable to perform the sort of work he would like to undertake with regard to the self and instead commits an action that is detrimental to the work he wishes to do. (2) There is a negative feeling attached to the cognitive assessment, "I am weak-willed." The agent reasons: "I have failed to work on that aspect of myself. I have been weak-willed." At that moment, the agent feels regret or feels some negative perturbation when he realizes that he is being *akratic*. There is a distinct feeling of moral failure. I now turn to examining some of the many colorations of this feeling.

We might say that the first inklings of possible *akratic* action appear when an agent senses inner conflict regarding some action that he or she is contemplating in undertaking. Phenomenologically it may feel as though the subject is being pulled apart by two different powers or forces. Some authors have described this feeling as "a tug of war" between two parts of the self.[44] And we may further notice that one force, in some sense, is already losing this tug of war: part of us is simply holding on, trying to prevent being pulled away by the other force.

Recovery is still possible, of course, even when we feel our will wavering. It is always possible to say: "No, I will not give into temptation, at least not today." But the feeling of wavering, of feeling oneself about to commit an action that goes against some work on the self that one wishes to do or conversely, some action that is perceived to be detrimental to the work that has already been undertaken *vis-a-vis* the self, is, I argue, yet another necessary condition for any weak-willed action.

There are also more nuanced feelings of wavering. Consider the phenomenological feeling of backsliding. What does it feel like to backslide? The feeling of backsliding seems to presuppose three things: (1) that one knows that one is not engaged in the actions one is meant to do. To feel that one is backsliding is to know that one is not committed to improving oneself, at least in the particular instance in question. To be sure, there may be a further sense that one needs to indulge in some activity that one had previously forsworn, but equally there is a sense that these reasons are really fallacious. (2) To backslide also seems to presuppose that one was acting in such a manner where the relationship one had to oneself was important, in need of improvement, and that such improvement was taking place. After all, to backslide presupposes that one is sliding from some forward position; at least some progress has been made. (3) There is also the feeling itself understood independently or minimally from whatever cognitive interpretation we might have of it. To feel that we are backsliding is to feel a sense of profound disappointment: it is to feel as though we are alienated from the project we sought to establish to and with ourselves.

To be *akratic* and to backslide presupposes that there is some sense of the improved self that remains present in the action. There is still some residual resistance to the action now taking place, but we feel overpowered by a dominant desire and therefore commit the action that is not in keeping

---

44. The classic description of this tug of war feeling between parts of the self is described in Plato's *Phaedo*. I examine this in greater detail below. For a more contemporary description of this tug of war feeling see, McGonigal, *The Willpower Instinct: How Self-Control Works*.

with the self we have projected. Weakness of will, in this context, is most akin to feeling overpowered.

Another feeling and example of "weakness of will" would be that of "caving." All that is present in this feeling is: (1) the desire to perform some action—an action that would seem to quench some inexorable thirst and, (2) there is a distinct feeling that some breaking point as occurred: where resistance within the agent completely breaks down and the agent, by his own lights, is dragged away by a desire as if he or she was a mere slave.[45] Some individuals have called such an experience as being on "auto-pilot" or viewing oneself from the outside like that of another. It is as if the agent no longer has the mental energy to pursue a particular course of action and becomes inclined to follow the desire in question. The individual is much like a dam where small leaks suddenly give way and the dam falls apart as a result of the force of the water behind it. The agent knows, at least initially, that he or she should perform a certain action, has the intention to do so, but is unable to put "rubber to the road" and, eventually, even the initial intention to perform some action dissolves.

What I think is interesting about this last course of akratic action is that there might not be a feeling of regret, at least attached to the action, in retrospect. The agent may deem that the intended action was unrealistic: the agent now believes that he or she never had the adequate energy to perform the intended action anyway or conversely to resist the temptation. Certainly in the case of caving we often provide ourselves with rationalizations that make us believe that we had no choice: we had to give in to temptation, or so we tell ourselves. This leads to an important question: "Is regret a necessary component for an action to be considered *akratic?*"

I would argue that regret is a necessary condition for *akratic* action. However, we must distinguish between two forms of regret: when there is clear regret in an action taken, I shall call this action-regret. Action-regret takes place when an agent regrets some action taken either because the agent deems that the action is regrettable in and of itself (perhaps the agent considers the action to be shameful) or because the action directly led to consequences that the agent believes to be regrettable, here construed as consequences that clearly do not conform with the agent's work-project.

The other feeling of regret I shall call character-regret. The agent regrets that he or she has a moral failing or some weakness—physical or

---

45. A reference to Plato's *Protagoras*. I will examine the slave analogy in more detail in chapter two.

psychical, etc.—such that he or she lacks the capacity to put a plan of character improvement into practice. With regard to weakness of will, I would claim that it is possible to lack action-regret and still be weak-willed: to be sure this would not mean that the action is not regrettable nor would it be morally neutral or morally praiseworthy, rather it is devoid of agential valuation. Certainly others may condemn the action, but the agent is of the opinion that the action was unavoidable; he was compelled to do it, though he did it freely. Action-regret, however, as result of temptation, is a sufficient condition for *akratic* action. When one feels regret that he or she has taken some action, that same individual understands that the action was avoidable and in some sense went against some fundamental core value of the self.

Character-regret is the other notion of regret I wish to speak to. Character regret is the regret one experiences when one commits an action and regrets that one is not strong enough to stop oneself from committing the said action. One regrets that perhaps the self is not edified enough to fend off some contrary desire to the self's project. Character regret explains why the auto-pilot example, where someone feels dragged off by some desire, is an example of *akrasia*, even though the individual believes that he or she had no control of his or her actions at that moment.

Character-regret also helps to explain why addiction is still akratic behavior. Some scholars have argued that true addiction is not akratic at all because it is compelled—the agent has no choice but to engage in the action he is about to take.[46] And if an action is compelled then we can't assign blame to an agent—which is precisely what we do when we call an agent weak-willed or an action weak-willed. It is for this reason that the above distinction is important: certainly the heroin addict knows that when he plunges the needle into his arm he is not performing worthwhile work on himself, but proceeds to insert the needle anyway. The addict may not experience action-regret believing that the action is unavoidable, but he or she experiences character-regret—he wishes he were not an addict. It is for this reason that addiction still falls under the umbrella of weakness of will.

So, what is *akrasia*? From the above discussion it was discovered that *akrasia*, at minimum, requires four components: (1) inner conflict; (2) the conflict stems from a desire that is contrary to some work that the self wishes to perform on itself because it has deemed such work to be important; (3) the agent has freedom to choose an alternative course of action; (4) the

46. See Mele, *Backsliding*.

individual experiences regret either because he is ashamed of the action taken, the action has led to regrettable consequences, or the individual regrets the weakness displayed by his character.

BRINGING THE FOUR QUESTIONS TOGETHER

When we refer to a weak-willed person, what exactly are we referring to? Are we referring to an agent, individual, person, mind, or subject? I believe that we normally think of the person at least minimally, as an individual, that is, as a singular entity. But one of the presuppositions of this position has to do with the word "entity." When we refer to an entity here we are presupposing that the entity exists in its singularity: there is an individuality, a distinctness to the thing in question. The entity is ontologically distinct from the world itself along with the things therein. But given this assumption the slackening of rule truly does not impact the entity's being. For the entity mysteriously stands beyond the actions it takes.

Further, such a view also assumes that the entity is ontologically robust; it is not simply a "place" or meeting ground for the interaction of real parts and components. For example, the word "mob" is not an individual entity, but rather a descriptor we give to the chaotic actions of a large group of people who have unlawfully assembled. Certainly a mob may seem to act with a singular purpose and intention: looting, behaving violently, etc., and it might also be the case that there is an event that has served to produce this mob and to fuel its anger. But it would be incorrect to claim that there is a slackening of "mob rule." A mob denotes a group of individuals who have no overarching purpose and certainly no end goal.

The above way of examining the notion of "slackening of rule" obviously differs for an *akratic* entity. For an *akratic* entity must have a purpose in invoking a rule or following an intention that appears to be in keeping with some deeply defined goal of itself. I have argued that each individual self has its own work-project. When an individual freely and knowingly acts to the detriment of his work project's fulfillment, that person is weak-willed and such a person experiences action-regret. If the individual freely and knowingly acts to the detriment of his work-project in a consistent and routine manner then that person is weak-willed and such a person experiences character-regret. My main argument thus far has been to show that it is the negative feelings we experience, such as regret, shame, guilt, etc., that highlight a weak-willed action or weak-willed relationship we have to ourselves.

The affective analysis of understanding weakness of will that I employ here cuts through the narrative we might use in order to rationalize an action that is not truly in our best considered interests. The problem with the traditional understanding of weakness of will, as demonstrated with Davidson's definition, is that one never comes to discover what is in one's best interest, all things considered, because one's best interest is already defined by a framework. And temptation, as we all know, employs its own framework when assessing the value of some object of desire. The notion of a work-project, the goal of improving the self, is one that we both cognitively and affectively understand. Negative perturbations, feelings of regret, shame, etc., that accompany actions give us a more intuitive and immediate understanding of when we are being weak-willed. The task of becoming strong-willed then is simply one of bringing one's self-undermining energies in line with one's self-edification project. As shown, there are many strategies as to how one might achieve this.

But before looking at how one might achieve realignment, as it were, regarding one's work-project and one's desires, one further objection to my position needs to be addressed. Some philosophers, such as Nietzsche for example, have argued that the self does not exist. The self is nothing more than a concoction of irrational drives. Thus the final task of this chapter will be to respond to this objection.

WHAT IF THE SELF IS NOTHING MORE THAN A CONSTELLATION OF MORE BASIC, PRE-EXISTING DRIVES?

According to Nietzsche, the self is nothing more than an assemblage: it is simply an expression of various drives which are housed in a body. Thus to speak of "self-choosing" or "self-desiring" is simply to associate some added thing, a self, with the desire. The self is something that is doubled in the explanation but does no causal explanatory work. All that is required to explain the "self" is a desire *sans* object or a drive. As Nietzsche explains in *On the Genealogy of Morals*:

> For, in just the same way as people separate lightning from its flash and take the latter as an *action*, as the effect of a subject which is called lightning, so popular morality separates strength from the

manifestations of strength, as if behind the strong person there were an indifferent substrate, which is *free* to express strength or not. But there is no such substrate; there is no "being" behind the doing, acting, becoming. "The doer" is merely made up and added into the action—the act is everything. People basically duplicate the action: when they see a lightning flash, that is an action of an action: they set up the same event first as the cause and then yet again as its effect.[47]

However, this notion of self, along with Nietzsche's answer to the question: "What governs our actions?" flies in the face of our most basic phenomenological experience. For it does appear that when we are metaphorically torn, when we are contemplating two very different actions, "we" exist in some neutral space: we are the ones contemplating two very different choices. Yet if this is right then we can separate the self even from one of its most cherished and deeply held desires. This could not be the case if the self was merely an afterthought, and expression of some desire.

Another problem with Nietzsche's notion of will as it relates to desire, temptation, and *akrasia* can be gleaned if we turn to an older translation of *akrasia* as "moral incontinence." Moral incontinence is analogous to physical incontinence. A person is physically incontinent if he is unable to control the movement of his bowels. In a similar vein, an individual is said to be morally incontinent when he cannot control his desires. This analogy seems to rest on several unquestioned assumptions. Firstly, when one is physically incontinent one feels "detached" from one's body. The body appears, phenomenologically speaking, as an alien vessel—our consciousness views certain bodily systems much as a captain might relate to a ship.[48] Where an individual once had an intimate control over his or her bowels, this control is now lost. In some sense, this feeling of control has been replaced with an overwhelming sense of alienation and loss.

Although I disagree with the ontological picture that the term moral incontinence seems to paint of *akrasia,* still there is something to this feeling of alienation. When we decide to fulfill a desire that comes upon us without warning and one with which we do not identify but one that leads

47. Nietzsche, *On the Genealogy of Morals,* GM 1:13.

48. This analogy, where we relate to our bodies as if we are merely the pilots or captains on a ship, is taken from Descartes' *Meditations VI.* There he claims that we have an intimate relation to our body. We do not simply relate to our body as if it were an unfeeling vessel. My point is that in some cases we do experience our body as a foreign or alien vessel. See Descartes, *Meditations on First Philosophy,* 64.

to action-regret once satisfied, then we feel that we are behaving against our true selves. Philosophers have named this experience "agent alienation."[49] Again it would seem that Nietzsche's identification of a desire with the subject, and the subject as nothing more as the rule given to a body politic, would entail that he would have a difficult time explaining such a feeling.

In keeping with the affective phenomenological goal of the work, we might do well to explore further this feeling of agent alienation. Certainly there are times where an individual does not feel quite himself with regard to some action just committed. Why does the agent feel alienated from his very action? He feels alienated because such an action goes against his most deeply cherished ideas he has regarding the relationship he has formed to himself. Such a feeling is anathema to the agent's defined work-project. For example, a moral agent, call him Bill, is not a drinker, in fact it is more accurate to say that he is a tee-totaller. Certainly Bill has been drunk in the past, but that was during his wild college years and those days are long behind him. Bill has not drunk for well over twenty years and has no desire to do so.

One night, purely on a whim, Bill decides to drive to a local bar and proceeds to get drunk, very drunk. He then chooses to drive. He is arrested and prosecuted for driving under the influence of alcohol. Bill has a difficult time explaining his behavior to his spouse, but an even more difficult time explaining his behavior to himself. He simply does not understand drunk, reckless, Bill. He understands that he is responsible for his actions because he remembers doing them, but the actions themselves are quite alien to him. Such a scenario is all too real for many persons and we might even be able to identify with Bill and recall similar incidences where actions taken on a whim led to "alien memories" and regrettable consequences.

We might generalize from the above scenario and claim that a slackening of rule occurs when the relationship of the self to the self breaks down as a result of some action. Agent-alienation is an extreme form of such a break down. But not all feelings of agent-alienation are examples of *akrasia*. It is possible, for example, to act with tremendous resolve in some situation or to do something truly commendable that runs counter to one's basic character.

There are other times, however, where an individual experiences the opposite feeling: agent-identification or pride. To feel pride is to feel a sense of accomplishment: it is to feel that one has accomplished what he or she

---

49. See Camus' *The Stranger*, for more on this sense of alienation.

has set out to achieve. With regard to the question then—"What rules?"—I would argue that instead of viewing the question as a metaphysical question (i.e., as a question about what the subject is), it is best to view the question from an affective state and ask: "When does a subject truly feel like a subject?" The answer: when the subject reflects on the feelings he has regarding some action taken. When does a subject feel that he has power or rule over himself? Again, the answer to this question, or so I would argue, is when the subject is able to carry out what he has identified as important character-edifying work. A subject who is able to edify himself in this way over an extended period of time is very often called "strong-willed."

When we think about a strong-willed individual we think that such an individual has resolve. What does it mean to have resolve? According to some philosophers it is simply this: to act on one's resolutions. This is a position that was first articulated by William Holton. He argues that strength of will is nothing more than not giving in to inclinations that run contrary to one's resolutions.[50] That is, one is strong willed if one holds to one's reasoned or well-considered resolutions, come what may. Weakness of will is the opposite: to be weak-willed is to give in to inclinations that run counter to our most reasoned resolutions; it is to break one's resolve too readily.

I accept this basic conceptual understanding of strong/weak willed characters, but argue that Holton has not fleshed out the emotive energies that feed and formulate those considered reasons that formulate a resolution. The answer to the question "What allows one to hold such resolutions?" is simply self-pride, very broadly construed. Self-pride is the answer to the "what rules?" question. Likewise, lack of self-pride is the answer to the question: "Why does a rule slacken?"

Self-pride is analogous, in at least some ways, to the pride one has in "a job well done." But it should be noted that self-pride is not co-extensive with one's profession or job. A doctor, for example, might take a lot of pride in saving lives and certainly he is right to feel proud as a result of his work, but he may nevertheless be weak-willed. The self-pride I am referring to goes much deeper than that. It is more akin to feeling self-approbation.

Self-approbation comprises both a meta-cognitive and emotive relationship to the self. From a meta-cognitive standpoint, to have self-approbation is to feel prideful with respect to the relationship one has to oneself. We speak, for example, of an individual who takes a great deal of pride in his or her work. A craftsman may take pride in creating artifacts: the

50. See Holton, *Willing, Wanting, Waiting*, 70.

artifacts are beautiful, durable, made of the finest materials, flawless, etc. In the same way, to be proud of the self is to be proud of all the actions that the self undertakes in order to establish the relationship that the self wishes to establish to itself.

One way to think of this relationship is to think of the self as a work of art, as an exercise of the self on the self. As Michel Foucault explains this relationship in his book *The Use of Pleasure*: "The essay—which should be understood as the assay or test by which, in the game of truth, one undergoes *changes*, and not as a simplistic appropriation of others for the purpose of communication—is the living substance of philosophy, at least if we assume that philosophy is still what it was in times past, i.e., an ascesis, askesis, an exercise of oneself in the activity of thought."[51] Foucault viewed this relationship of the self to the self *(rapport a soi)* in aesthetic terms: the self is free to relate to itself in whatever terms it establishes for itself. As Foucault suggests in "On the Genealogy of a Work in Progress": "Why . . . couldn't everyone's life become a work of art?"[52]

For the purposes of this book, I would like to appropriate Foucault's notion of *askesis*, but to untie it from its aesthetic moorings and to anchor it instead to emotive or affective weights.[53]

SO, WHAT HAS BEEN LEARNED?

The question "What rules?" is best answered by turning to the emotive question: "When does a subject feel most like a subject?" The answer to this question, if one recalls, was: when there is a feeling of self-approbation. The feeling of self-approbation gives way when an individual is weak-willed: the individual experiences action-regret or character-regret with respect to some action chosen. The relationship the individual has to himself is undermined; the control the agent normally exhibits is less predictable. In contrast, when we claim that someone is strong-willed we mean to say the relationship she has to herself is such that it is unlikely to change. Notice that the behavior of the individual might change, but it is in accordance with some overall plan that seeks to establish further the goal

51. Foucault, *The History of Sexuality Volume II*, 9. Italics mine.

52. Foucault, "On The Genealogy of Ethics: An Overview of a Work in Progress," 350. I have examined Foucault's new aesthetic-ethical model of self-relationship extensively in several articles and books.

53. While Foucault's position is interesting I believe it is untenable.

of self-approbation. This relationship, I argue, is one that is strengthened according to the two tethers of cognitive and affective reflection. Both of these mooring lines are required in order to truly experience self-pride. And it should also be noted that they are not separate lines: cognition can come to influence how we feel and vice versa, as Elster showed.

In the next chapter, I will investigate Plato's early attempt to explain *akrasia*. In brief, Socrates argues that *akrasia* does not exist; one is simply intellectually deficient. I will examine Plato's *Protagoras*, and *Meno* in order to flesh out what is often referred to as Socrates' moral intellectualism position. A moral intellectualist position is one that holds that it is reason, all by itself, that can come to affect character change. Obviously if this position is true, then my thesis is false. I demonstrate that the middle Plato clearly had some difficulty in holding such a moral intellectualist position and, as a result, Plato changes his view dramatically in *Republic*.

Chapter Two

Is Weakness of Will Even Real?

Plato's Early Account of Akrasia
in *Protagoras* and *Meno*

IN CHAPTER ONE, I investigated the problem of *akrasia* in rather broad brush strokes. My purpose in that chapter was to examine the components of akratic behavior and more specifically to answer the broader question: "What is *akrasia*?" I showed that *akrasia* may be viewed from four interpolated perspectives. I then examined the different ways in which one might interpret these components. Finally, I examined several clear examples of akratic behavior like backsliding and caving and identified what I thought to be the key affective aspects to these experiences. It is now time, however, to pare back and provide a more thorough conceptual analysis of this investigation. I now intend to investigate whether *akrasia* is possible.

This is an important and necessary analysis because my overall argument thus far is that *akrasia* is an affective relationship that characterizes the self's relationship to itself. If, however, this affective characterization was found to be a conceptual misunderstanding—if *akrasia* does not exist—then my thesis would be false.

Plato's early theory of *akrasia*, as presented in *Protagoras* and *Meno*, presents the position that *akrasia* is incoherent: if an agent is free to choose between two choices then he will pick whichever choice he calculates to be in his best interest. Following other scholars in the field, I will call Plato's early account of *akrasia*, Socrates' account, as the position is a reductionist account of *akrasia* and is evinced by the character Socrates in Plato's early dialogues.[1] Plato's later position, as developed in the middle period, I shall call Plato's account of *akrasia*. It too is evinced by the character Socrates, but it is very clear that in the dialogues *Phaedo* and *Republic* (two central dialogues of Plato's middle period) Plato does hold that *akratic* actions are real.

In this chapter I explain, analyze, and document Socrates' justification for *akrasia* along with how his position changes from *Protagoras* to *Meno*. In chapter three, I then develop Plato's account of *akrasia* in his middle works.

In brief, Socrates argues that *akrasia* does not stem from being weak-willed, but from being weak-minded. As such, feelings have no role to play in terms of explaining how *akrasia* is possible nor do they have any part in preventing it. *Akrasia* occurs because one has mismeasured, period, end of story. However, this account must not have been very satisfying as Plato in *The Republic* clearly demonstrates that non-rational desires may, at times, overpower reason. In chapter three, I explain Plato's more mature understanding of *akrasia* and demonstrate how his account supports my initial affective thesis.

Accordingly, I have three objectives in this chapter: (1) to explain Socrates' account of *akrasia* such that I present the position in the strongest terms possible; (2) to show that there are several flaws with the position; and (3) to demonstrate how the account begins to shift ever so slightly in Plato's *Meno*. I argue that this shifting continues in Plato's middle dialogues—namely, the *Phaedo* and *Symposium*—until we have the final and much improved explanation of *akrasia* as given in *Republic*.

Before examining the dialogue *Protagoras* in more considered detail, and more specifically the argument that Socrates advances to show that *akrasia* is impossible, I will first explain Socrates' argument against *akrasia* as succinctly as I can. Briefly stated here, Socrates evinces that those who commit bad actions (whether construed as evil, immoral, ill-advised, etc.) do so because they are confused about what the right or good thing to do is in a given context. So called *akratic* individuals, Socrates continues, lack cognitive power, not will power: individuals commit moral mistakes because they truly do not know any better, *simpliciter*. However, this

---

1. For two very different of articles on Socrates' account of *akrasia* see, Perrin, "A Defense of Socrates' Denial of Akrasia," and Woolf, "Consistency and Akrasia in Plato's Protagoras."

interpretation of *akratic* action serves to dissolve it as a coherent concept: *akrasia,* as weakness of will, does not exist. Why? Because will does not move us to a particular object. Will plays no causal role whatsoever when it comes to understanding the real forces that move human beings towards or away from objects or experiences. It is rather reason and desire—or more accurately, interests (a fusion of reason and desire)—that act as the true engines of the soul. We make mistakes, moral or otherwise, because we have mismeasured: we have made a calculative error. We reasoned that one choice would provide more pleasure, for example, than that of another, but now only realize that such a choice brings with it more suffering. It is our reason that is responsible for making such mistakes.

Socrates begins his argument by entertaining the common view of *akratic* action. An *akratic* action, according to what Socrates calls the "common view," holds the following: an agent, say Tom, knows that choice X is better than choice Y, but chooses, because of a multitude of factors (because of either temptation, fear, or anger), Y. Nevertheless, this description of *akrasia,* Socrates extols, cannot be correct: for if the said individual really knew that X was better than Y then he would have chosen X. Because this did not happen then some other reason (and not a desire) prevented the individual from making the right choice. That reason, so claims Socrates, is ignorance; the agent is truly ignorant with regard to which is the better choice. Socrates identifies *akrasia* not with spiritual deficiency, but with cognitive deficiency. In *Protagoras* he expounds on this new explanation to explain, what appears at first sight, to be weak-willed actions.

If Socrates denies the existence of *akrasia* does he then deny the existence of immoderate individuals—individuals who are prone to a life of vice? Of course not! Obviously there are individuals who seem to follow vice instead of virtue. What Socrates would deny is the traditional explanation given to explain this phenomenon, namely, weakness of will. The common view might hold that such individuals are immoderate, meaning that they have little control over their desires. Such immoderation is explained, again, according to the "many" or "common" as a character flaw; but it this explanation that Socrates rejects. Instead Socrates argues that such individuals suffer from weakness of *intellect:* they are unable to make proper judgments.

Given this rather short explanation of Socratic weakness of will, we might think that Socrates' basic notion is no longer compatible with *akrasia,* at least traditionally defined. This is true. For Socrates, one always chooses what one deems to be best. However, we should notice that the basic idea of *akrasia that I have argued for* is still consistent with Socrates' theory provided that we reinterpret what it means to be "without power." For Socrates, to be "without power" means to lack reason such that one is prone to committing actions that are not in the agent's considered best interest when viewed *post facto*. One cannot choose Y knowing that Y is not the best course of action. My position suggests that the idea of being without power is best viewed as a feeling: it is best understood as a basic subjective relationship that one has to the self. It is marked by a general feeling that one does not, or cannot usually or typically, follow through on one's intentions. For example, one may feel powerless to overcome an addiction to sugary treats or one does not have the energy to start the exercise program that one acknowledges one should start, etc. This is the initial feeling of weakness of will, and a subject who so experiences this feeling is weak-willed, at least according to her own lights. So, instead of focusing on the basic feeling of the possible free actions that the agent has available to herself within a given context as the fundamental relationship of subjectivity, which is what I argue, Socrates instead would emphasize reason, and more specifically the capacity of the agent to understand what is really in her best interests, all things considered. This entails that Socrates accepts the basic idea which purports that we act in accordance with what we believe to be in our own best interest, but denies that it is possible to act against this perception, provided that one is free to do so.

What does it mean to say that an action is not in an agent's considered best interest? This is but one of the deep and perplexing issues that revolve around Socrates' restatement of the *akratic* problem. Certainly it is a problem that we encountered, albeit very briefly, in chapter one when I examined Davidson's understanding of *akrasia*. Since this chapter is concerned to examine the conceptual aspects of *akrasia*, it is now time to examine this perplexing statement here. One reading would seem to suggest that Socrates' view of "best interest" in *The Protagoras* is to equate considered self-interest with egotistic self-interest or whatever affords the agent the most pleasure. It is unlikely that Socrates is here advocating what might be termed psychological hedonism, though such a view has been defended in the secondary literature.[2] Rather, he uses hedonism as the common view of

2. See Hackforth, "Hedonism in Plato's Protagoras." Hackforth writes: "How are we to know when we mistake an apparent Good for a real good? Plato's first attempt to answer this question was that of Psychological Hedonism. . . . He soon advanced beyond this view." Ibid., 42.

action taken up by the *hoi polloi*. He takes up the view of the common in order to show that being overcome by pleasure, as the common view has it, is irreparably incoherent. Obviously to think of reason as a mere "pleasure calculator" is not Socrates' fully developed position on the subject. For Socrates, reason—or more aptly put knowledge—is equated with reaching the Good or Virtue, but while this position is implied in the early dialogues it is not fully developed until Plato's middle period.[3] In any case, rule then, at least construed here, simply denotes the considered judgment of reason as regards some action. If one is rational then one follows the rule of reason, which has calculated the course of action an individual should take in order for said individual to be afforded maximal pleasure.

Socrates does not spend any time outlining precisely what the Good truly entails and instead proceeds to argue, at least for most of the dialogue, against the reality or modal possibility of the term "being overcome by pleasure." Accordingly, the dialogue also gives the reader one of the first articulations of hedonism in Western history.

Hedonism is the ethical position that states that human beings are motivated to pursue pleasure and avoid pain. Pain and pleasure are the true motivators of the human psyche, and as such, are the true sources that underpin all action. This model of human action is termed psychological hedonism, in contrast to, say, physical hedonism, because some heavy lifting has be done on the part of the psyche: for it is the psyche, very broadly construed at this point, that is responsible for assessing some action. In other words, it is the psyche that is responsible for assessing the desirability of some action or object over that of another. Psychological hedonism purports to explain why we crave objects and indulge appetites that are inherently bad for the body such as addictive narcotics, for example. It is the mind that has placed determinate values on objects—not the body.

Now, turning to the dialogue, what is perhaps interesting about *Protagoras* is that the method of question and answer (elenchus) that Socrates usually employs in the early dialogues is altered here. For instance, in the early Platonic dialogues, such as *The Euthyprho* and *The Laches*, Socrates' dialogue represents the main substantive points of Plato's philosophy. Indeed Euthyprho, as a character, appears as a literary device present only to advance the philosophical plot—he really has nothing substantial to

---

3. This seems to be the majority scholarly view on the subject. See Dyson, "Knowledge and Hedonism in Plato's Protagoras" and Zeyl, "Socrates and Hedonism: Protagoras 351b–358d," for representative arguments that support the anti-hedonist position.

contribute to the philosophical discussion regarding the nature of piety. This is even more true for the character, Meno. Meno's bizarre definitions of virtue appear to be only "jumping off points" for Socrates' rather protracted and, sometimes, "tangential" discussions on the nature of virtue.[4]

The Protagoras is very different from these other dialogues. The dialogue begins in a typical early Platonic fashion by having the principal interlocutor about whom the dialogue is entitled to state his position before Socrates offers his refutation. But there are two profound differences: first Protagoras is a philosopher in his own right. He has original and insightful views on virtue, the nature of rationality, and indeed on weakness of will. Protagoras' own views—or at least the views that can be reconstructed from Plato's portrayal of the great philosopher in the dialogue of the same name—will be explored as we investigate the dialogue in greater detail. Secondly, the mechanics of the dialogue are also very different from that of previous dialogues: towards the middle of the dialogue, both Protagoras and Socrates are "thinking together" as it were and in so doing both contribute to a very new ethical position. Indeed, in some parts, Plato would appear to be advancing his own philosophic stance from the mouth of Protagoras only then to have Socrates affirm and deepen the initial position. This can be clearly seen in the lines prior to section 352 (in which Socrates articulates his unique and powerful view on *akrasia*) where the dialogue concerns the nature of reason. Both are on the same side of the debate in holding that nothing within the human being is more powerful than reason. Their disagreement has to do with the view of reason held by "the many" or "popular opinion."[5]

This disagreement with popular opinion revolves around incontinence. Protagoras and Socrates alike are of the opinion that people do not knowingly commit bad actions. Reason, in other words, is the most powerful force we possess as human beings and can neither be overcome by passion nor driven underground by fear. Protagoras claims in this regard: "It would be shameful indeed for me above all people to say that wisdom and knowledge are anything but the most powerful forces in human activity." Socrates replies: "Right you are."[6]

---

4. Interestingly, *The Meno* has become best known for one of its tangential discussions: the slave-boy dialogue.

5. The topic of *akrasia* appears on line 352A of *Protagoras*.

6. Plato, *Protagoras*, 352a, 782.

But as the dialogue proceeds, they both realize that this is the minority view. Most people, they argue, assume that wisdom is powerless when it is suddenly overcome by pleasure. Socrates states:

> What do you think about knowledge? Do you go along with the majority or not? Most people think this way about it, that it is not a powerful thing, neither a leader nor a ruler. They do not think of it in that way at all; but rather in this way: while knowledge is often present in a man, what rules him is not knowledge but rather anything else—sometimes anger, sometimes pleasure, sometimes pain, at other times often fear.[7]

It is tempting to think that Socrates will claim that the individual's will is analogous to the rule of a state. For just as a political state is constituted by warring factions, so too, a person is simply a constitution of warring drives: some of the drives are for pleasure, some seek retribution (anger), and others are drives to flight (fear). One might then believe that Socrates holds that to rule rightly is to rule each of these warring states, with their very different agendas and goals, with reason. But this is not an accurate model of Plato's early position. Instead, Socrates comes to extoll the view that reason is the sole motivator behind human action.

The many, however, do not think of the individual in this way at all. They believe that the individual is led by temporary rulers: "sometimes pleasure . . . sometimes fear, etc." In fact, reason is not a leader at all. Socrates puts this last point most forcefully with his much discussed metaphor of slavery. Socrates says: "They think of his knowledge as being utterly dragged around by all these other things as if it were a slave."[8]

Fleshing out this common view to explain human action, namely, that of hedonism, seems to rest on two points. The first is that the root of action is not reason at all, but a non-rational desire. Such a desire is not irrational because this qualifier connotes a desire that would be contrary to reason, and we do not have enough evidence to make this claim. The desire is non-rational because reason cannot change the direction of such a desire. The desire is immune to whatever powers reason possesses. At best, reason may be summoned to help one achieve the end of some desire, but reason cannot alter the basic thrust of the desire—only another, more powerful desire can do that.

---

7. Plato, *Protagoras*, 352b-c, 782.
8. Plato, *Protagoras*, 352 b-c 782.

The second point we may take away from this brief discussion concerns the metaphor that Socrates employs, which depicts reason as a slave. Now an initial reading of this passage might suggest that reason is simply powerless *simpliciter* when it comes to desire. Just as slaves are powerless when confronted by their master, so too, the metaphor suggests, reason is powerless when confronted by a desire to which it finds itself in opposition. However, there are a number of other ways to read this passage, for we might also supplement this reading with the line "being utterly dragged around . . . ." If reason had no power then why would a desire drag it around in the first place? Consider for a moment why a master employs a slave. A master may drag a slave to a designated spot so that the slave can perform some task. Slaves are useful in so far as they can work toward some end. In the same way, reason has at least some power because it would appear that whatever desire is master at the time requires reason's services. Thus, a desire drags reason around presumably to perform some sort of work.

If this interpretation is correct then there is some measure of power that reason has, even according to those who hold the "common-view." Reason is required in order to obtain the object the individual desires just as a master requires a servant to perform some task. The master will not, or perhaps cannot, perform the task on his own. Just as the master requires a slave or slaves because there are limits on his time, energy, or even knowledge, so too, it is acknowledged desire is limited.

We may add to this interpretation, however. A master employs a slave for some purpose. A slave is an instrument, a tool for some design, some agenda. Thus, in the same manner, desire cannot be satisfied without also employing a tool. This tool, is, of course, reason. From this point begins Socrates' *reductio ad absurdum* against the common view. The point of this *reductio* is to force the common view holders of *akrasia* to concede that reason is not powerless after all and, more to the point, to prove that reason has power over desire, in that a desire cannot be satisfied in the absence of reason. Socrates will then build on this to show that, in fact, reason cannot even be a slave to desire, but is in fact the master. I will explain how this *reductio* works below, but before I do there is yet another interpretation of this metaphor that deserves a closer look.

Another interpretation of this metaphor suggests that a master could drag a slave around for the sole purpose of displaying his power: it is the exercise of power itself that is pleasurable and therefore desirable. Under this interpretation, the means of power is itself the goal. From the standpoint of this reading, the relations of power between a master and his servant are not established for the sake of utility—the servant is not simply the "arm of the master"; the master does not simply use the slave to obtain some object or to complete some project. Rather, it is the feeling of control for its own sake that is the true pleasure.

What would such an interpretation entail? It would mean that the servant's very subjugation is in itself desirable. If we cash out this metaphor in terms of inserting reason into the place of the slave and desire in the place of the master, it would mean that reason's power is not an intrinsic capacity of the human being. Rather the power of reason is something that is relative to the desire of desire. The servant has some degree of power, but only because the master is pleased with the current relationship of subjugation. Exploring this interpretation in more detail we may then believe that reason here, as the analogue for the servant, is at the mercy of desire, i.e., the master, desire, is so powerful that it has no use for reason and drags reason around with it because there is some pleasure in corrupting what is thought to be incorruptible. Further analysis, however, will reveal that his conclusion is unwarranted: reason's efficacy cannot be so easily eliminated.

To be sure one might question this strong reading and suggest that "the many" only claim that whatever task reason is performing can be negated at the slightest whim by a desire or fears. Thus, the metaphor only shows that a superior power to that of reason can always supplant an agent's reasoned intention. But I would argue, and I think this is borne out in what follows, that what the many mean to say is that reason is both overcome by some superior passion, drive, or what have you *and* that reason is made use of just as a slave is made use of by his master. Reason is employed in the service of some desire and desire in some sense desires to subjugate reason. This again seems to be concordant with the phenomenological evidence on hand. If we give full play to the position of the many, it does appear that when we are overcome by pleasure we need reason to put pleasure's agenda in motion in two senses. Firstly, the pursuit of some object of pleasure very often requires a detailed series of steps and actions. Reason is required in order to fulfill these steps. And secondly in another way too, when we are overcome by pleasure it seems that we rationalize why it might be a good idea to allow the object of pleasure to overcome us. This rationalization, however, would be after the fact—the desire has already overcome us, at least to some extent, and now uses reason as a further force to convince "us" to place rubber to the road (whatever that "us" might be).

What the many argue, at least as I charitably reconstruct Socrates' understanding of the common view is as follows: we are not overcome by pleasure after all. Instead we are attempting to justify our post-pleasure mental state which has caused us to alter our view of our previous pre-pleasure intentions, which we now come to discover may or may not be grounded on well-reasoned propositions. And if all this is correct then incontinence is impossible. It is impossible to have the choice and ability to do Y, to know that Y is the best choice when all things are considered, and yet to perform X at the time when we commit the action. It is possible, of course, to interpret the action after the fact as an action taken out of incontinence. But when we in fact act in a way where we desire pleasure we do so because we feel that such an action is the best course of action to take, all things considered. Where X here is that which is desired because it affords us pleasure, the desire is buttressed by a rationalization. Reason is not powerless when it comes "face to face" with an appetite, rather, one reasoned intentioned has acquiesced when confronted with a "better" reasoned intention.

Fleshing out Socrates' brilliant reasoning in more detail, the first part of Socrates' argument is to show that the theory of action accepted by most average men, namely hedonism, requires calculation. Hedonism holds that individuals seek pleasure and avoid pain. But both pleasure and pain are infused with cognition: the individual must understand how to weigh actions such that more pleasure will befall the individual in the long-run. Pleasures and pains alike are weighed by an individual according to the dictates of a calculus of which reason assesses.

This position might seem similar if not the same as Jeremy Bentham's utilitarianism.[9] But utilitarianism is a more robust position than the one that is espoused by the many in Socrates' day. For Bentham argued that we should pursue our natural instinct, which is for pleasure, and that is not what is being articulated here. All the many claim is that we do in fact act according to certain desires. Reason, whether we wish it or not, is simply a calculator for our base desires. The "many's" argument does not purport to be a normative argument at all, but descriptive; it describes what we do as human beings, not what we should do. Indeed, it is for this reason that the many describe the pursuit of vice as *akratic*—desire leads reason away kicking and screaming.

9. See Bentham, *An Introduction to the Principles of Morals and Legislation*.

Socrates begins his demonstration by providing examples of painful practices and situations that have a pleasurable benefit in the long-run. Socrates says:

> You who say that some painful things are good, do you not say that such things as athletics and military training and treatments by doctors such as cautery, surgery, medicines, and starvation diet are good things, though painful? Would they say so? Yes. Would you call these things good for the reason that they bring about intense pain and suffering, or because they ultimately bring about health and good condition of bodies and preservation of cites and power over others and wealth? Would they agree?
> Yes.
> These things are good only because they result in pleasure and in relief and avoidance of pain? Or do you have some other criterion in view other than pleasure and pain, on the basis of which you would call these things good? They say no, I think.[10]

Socrates' argument, in this respect, seeks to do two things. First, Socrates evinces that the hedonist is incorrect: we are not solely driven by pleasure *simpliciter*. To claim that we are is to hold that human beings, essentially, are driven to act from pure appetite. Let us call this position the pure appetite theory. Socrates' claim is to show that appetites must be evaluated, and in order for an appetite to be evaluated reason is required. Socrates' answer to the question "What drives us to act?" is the answer, what is good for us overall. This is an answer that must hold true, Socrates shows, even for the hedonist. Now Socrates himself has his own views on what the Good is and he gives us a glimpse of this in the dialogue, but for now, he wishes to concentrate on what the many think is good. And clearly what the many think to be good is the pursuit of pleasure, period. Second, Socrates will then show that if the human subject is not driven by pleasure alone then he cannot be overcome by it either. Thus the "many" are simply mistaken when they claim that one acts badly because he or she is "overcome" by pleasure; they do not understand the true motivational forces behind the soul. According to the common view, one can only be overcome—in the way "being overcome by something" is being employed here—by some contrary desire.

However, it is this very point that Socrates attacks without mercy. To desire is to desire some object, but to desire some thing, indeed anything,

10. Plato, *Protagoras*, 354A-B, 783.

is to know something about that thing. Desire by itself cannot pursue what it desires without knowing something about the object of desire. Indeed, without reason, desire could not even differentiate its preferences or distinguish one object from another. Reason is not simply a tool that desire uses in order to pursue some object. In fact, without reason, desire would be incomprehensible to itself for it would not understand what it desires.

Moreover, when we compare two desires in order to determine which desire we shall pursue, we do so by weighing the advantages and disadvantages of each object of desire. But to weigh is to evaluate and to evaluate is to use reason. Thus, all pursuits of desirable objects are infused with reason: there is no way to get around this.

We can see this next step in Socrates' argument here:

> Well then my good people: Since it has turned out that our salvation in life depends on the right choice of pleasures and pains, be they more or fewer, greater or lesser, farther or nearer, doesn't our salvation seem first of all to be measurement which is the study of relative excess and deficiency and equality?
> It must be.
> And since it is measurement, it must definitely be an art, and knowledge.
> They will agree.[11]

The upshot of this analysis is this: it is seemingly impossible to be overcome by passion, for to be directed by passion is to be directed by an evaluation: "this object is desirable, I want it, or this object is more desirable than this one, I therefore choose it." This is an evaluation of the merits of an object. Furthermore to measure two choices one must understand the merits of each choice and measure each of these merits against each other. All of this requires judgment and therefore requires reason. Reason cannot be a mere slave to passion, but is an equal partner.

So what then is Socrates' explanation of *akratic* action? It is as follows: as long as we accept the hedonist interpretation of human action combined with Socrates' notion of measurement, we can explain *akratic* action thusly: mistakes are made because we have failed to make the correct measurement. We believe that some object is desirable now, but realize only upon acquiring said object that we mismeasured: we have gone against our own rule of pursuing that which is most pleasurable. We have opted for a lesser pleasure instead of a greater one. By way of analogy, *akrasia* can be

11. Plato, *Protagoras*, 357B, 787.

explained in terms of measuring distance: just as we think that something is small in the distance, but becomes larger as we get closer, so too we may think that indulging in a desire will have a negligible consequence now when in fact the consequences will become more pressing as time passes.

SOCRATES AND PROMETHEUS: IS ANYTHING TRULY MEASURABLE?

Socrates' reduction, while powerful, does have some serious flaws. I now wish to examine some of the problems with Socrates' argument. One of the lynchpins of the argument is the idea that all things can be measured and that all things may be measured by the same metric. But this is questionable. For first, it is questionable that all fulfillment of desire can be measured. To argue for this conclusion is to suggest that there is only one value for any given thing. The notion that an action may be a "mixed bag" is refuted from the get-go. Given the model that Socrates supposes, it may be impossible to accept such an objection. After all, any example given the hedonist model is measurable and therefore reducible to one form of measurement. But what if the very notion of pleasure being infused with reason was rejected? What if one challenged Socrates' very "promethean" way of thinking?

Promethean thinking is named after Prometheus the Titan, enemy of the Greek gods and creator of man in Greek mythology. Prometheus was responsible for giving fire to humankind but also the ability to reason. Prometheus is usually given the title of "forethought"—he thinks before he acts. This type of thinking is thought to be a virtue: it is important to think through the consequences of an action before committing to the action. Certainly the Greeks exalted this type of thinking as it was one of, if not the chief personality trait of Odysseus, a paragon of Greek excellence.[12]

Continuing with the paragon of Promethean thinking, namely Odysseus, we discover that Odysseus does many things that are not exactly rational. For example, Odysseus has his men bind him to the mast of his ship just as they are about to sail pass the dreaded Sirens.[13] The Sirens are creatures with melodic voices that lure sailors to the shore. Sailors are so entranced by such voices that they do not realize the true nature of these creatures before it is too late: the Sirens are really monsters who have a great appetite for human flesh. Odysseus is curious about these creatures,

12. See Miller, "The Promethean Story in Plato's Protagoras."
13. See Homer, *The Odyssey*, Chapter XII.

despite his better judgment: he desires to hear their music to see why so many men have found them impossible to resist. He commands all his men to place wax in their ears so that they won't be able to hear the songs of these creatures. But Odysseus has his men bind him to the mast so that he can hear the melodious songs and if in fact he is subject to these creatures' charms, he will not be able to act on them: he will be prevented from following the creatures to his certain doom. Odysseus is enthralled by such creatures and struggles to free himself from the mast. He orders his men to cut him down, but because they cannot hear him, he is ignored. Eventually, Odysseus and his ship sail past the creatures.[14]

Odysseus' desire to hear the songs of the Sirens and yet not succumb to their trap is a calculated risk: he wants to have his cake and not be eaten too! But notice that this image with Odysseus bound exposes the true powerlessness of reason: reason is helpless in the face of desire after all! For a truly rational person would steer clear of the Sirens or would ensure that his ears were also plugged, for the risk clearly does not equal the reward. Odysseus, instead, uses all his reasoning abilities, all his strategizing, to devise a plan to satisfy an irrational desire and not suffer the usual painful consequences.

It is commonplace to refer to this thinking as "instrumental" since rationality itself is considered to be no more than a giant calculator of sorts. But one of the issues with this sort of thinking is that it, by itself, cannot determine the proper ends of action. We calculate a course of action in order to satisfy some desire, but why we perform the calculation is a mystery; it is beyond our rationality. Even if we are a perfectly rational Odysseus and plug our ears when we pass the Siren's island, it is still rational to ask, "For what purpose?" Is it better to live a longer life with fewer rich experiences than to live a short life full of profound, wondrous, and seminal encounters? Reason by itself cannot determine which of these choices is to be preferred. At some point, it is desire, *simpliciter,* which makes the choice and then has reason calculate the path such that the desire can be fulfilled.

Socrates' view or at least the implicit view he adopts for the purposes of the *Protagoras* is to suggest that desire pushes reason to perform the correct calculation. Reason is essential in desire's determination of the value of an object, but reason, while not a slave, remains a cog in a more elaborate machine that cannot be truly understood. This criticism of reason in the *Protagoras* has been commented on by other thinkers in the secondary

14. See, Homer, *The Odyssey*, chapter XII.

literature. This criticism, as we will see below, undermines any autonomy that Socrates sought to give to reason in the first place.[15]

In any case, rationality *simpliciter* is adopted by Socrates as the only means for thinking and desiring—all desiring is shot through with an instrumental rationality, for to desire one thing is always to desire it more than something else. To desire some object or experience more than another is a primitive way of measuring the feeling of desire that we have. The self then is always deeply conflicted—it always has conflicting desires. The question is whether this phenomenological feeling is learned or innate. If it is innate and unassailable then Socrates' position goes through. If it is not innate but learned then it can be unlearned.

In contrast, one might claim that we might do well to pit Epimethean thinking against Promethean thinking. Epimetheus, in Greek mythology, was the brother of Prometheus and was responsible for distributing all the natural talents of animals at the creation of the world. Such gifts included fur, sharp teeth, claws, wings, etc. But when Epimetheus distributed such gifts he did not give much forethought to the way in which such gifts were being handed out. When he ran out of claws and teeth, for example, he gave creatures slender legs and wings so as to escape the animals that were given these terrible instruments of death.[16] It is for this reason that Epimetheus is given the name "afterthought"—he does not think through his actions and must make adjustments to his ill-conceived previous actions. Certainly the Greeks would think of afterthought as a vice—we see that Odysseus is greatly admired precisely because he is crafty: he strategizes and ponders considerably the course of action he will take before he takes it.

Be that as it may, one could argue that if we think of desire in this Epimetheus sense then it might avoid Socrates' charge that all desiring is already laced with fore-thought and thus measurement. An Epimethean, in contrast to a Promethean, might simply act on a whim: he simply avoids calculation as best one can and follows what desire takes his fancy. While one could not always act on a whim, in all situations, nevertheless, cultivating such an art would have its own advantages in that one's life would not be subject to the fascist dictates of instrumental rationality.

15. See Naas, "Philosophy Bound: The Fate of the Prometheus Socrates." Naas argues that Promethean thinking is inseparable from, and therefore in some way dependent on, Epimethean (afterthought) thinking.

16. See Graves, *The Greek Myths*, 39.

Promethean rationality is the view that Socrates is espousing. He argues that pleasure is measurable and can be calculated. And if this is correct then there will be some who are better at performing these calculations than others. But if this is the case then a craft of pleasure-calculation is possible. Those who are the best at pleasure calculation are philosophers because only they can foresee the full measurement of some action. It is as if such philosophers, to use Socrates sight metaphor, are far-sighted whereas everyone else is near-sighted.

Thus Socrates' position will appeal to those who have already taken the promethean turn—those who are so inclined to stop and assess a desire even when the desire is in the process of being fulfilled. The individual is entrapped within the confines of measuring to such a degree that it is impossible to view the object as it is presented immediately at hand—the individual is always viewing the object in terms of future consequences.

The objection articulated here, namely, that promethean thinking may just be one of at least two frameworks that one could choose to employ as one lives one's life leads to another problem for Socrates: just because the indulgence of some present pleasure will produce more harm in the future does not mean that whatever value we give to it in the present is automatically devalued now. To see this point, imagine the following scenario of Sally the stalwart investor. Sally decides to invest 20 percent of her salary from the time she has her first career say, at 25, until the time she retires. Sally has some very good reasons for investing. She reasons that people are living longer and she wants to enjoy her golden years without worrying about getting a part-time job when she retires to make ends meet. She has plans that she would like to fulfill: such as travelling around the globe and so forth. Such an expedition will be a rather costly affair for Sally, but it is a trip that Sally has always desired to go on. Sally calculated this trip as best she can and believes that such an excursion will cost upward of $100,000 by the time she retires.

Sally is now age sixty-five and has followed through on her investment plans. She has accumulated quite a nest egg. But should she convert her retirement investments into a livable pension? According to Socrates' reasoning the answer is a clear no. Although Sally might like to take that trip around the world, it is also possible that she might suffer from some costly life-threatening illness in the years to come. Since cancer rates rise with an individual's age, there is a significant chance that Sally will be more prone to acquiring some malignant cancer as she gets older.[17] Treatment for such a disease will be costly. Sally might do better to save her money so that she will be able to afford the costly treatments when or if such an event happens. This conclusion would seem to be the most sensible given Socrates' way of thinking.

It is important to notice that Sally does not know how long she will live and thus does not know the true measure of the cost of the trip. According to Socrates' reasoning, though she has prepared an itemized list of all expenses, the expense of the trip cannot be measured in terms of these expenses alone for we do not know what we might have to give up in the future if we take the trip now. Sally might need this extra $100,000 because she may end up living more years than she initially thought she would. Or she may need the extra money because she believes that nursing home costs will rise substantially in the next decade and this money could be used to allow her to live in relative comfort for these remaining years. What's more, all these reasons clearly outweigh the value that Sally herself gives to the trip. Yes it is her life-long dream to take the trip but she would rather be in a high quality nursing home towards the end of her life than to be "warehoused" in a minimal care, squalid, facility.

The point we may take away from this discussion is this: nothing is truly measurable, for the means of measurement are neither given in the present nor in the unforeseeable future. They are never given at all. Socrates' position is deeply problematic precisely because of the manner in which he has reinterpreted hedonism. Hedonism for Socrates does not mean: always seek to attain maximum pleasures. Socrates' hedonism is the position that holds that we should always maximize our best interests. Returning to Sally, her overall best interest might very well be preparing to live in a physical and mental state without pain in her not so golden years. And because we cannot predict what our maximum interests might be in the future, we seem to be forced into the position of denying what pleasures can be afforded in the here and now. Since it is always possible to accrue more of what we value by failing to engage in some vice or even whim, Socrates counsels that we should always wait. Yet such a position does seem to be solely motivated by worry, not reason. While reason may not be a slave to pleasure or fear, it now becomes a slave to anxiety.

To return to Socrates' argument, after showing that the hedonist really seeks to maximize his best interests and not just base pleasure, Socrates

17. See "Cancer Incidence by Age," Cancer Research UK.

demonstrates that the same analysis may also work to explain the common view of rash acts. The many claim that most rash acts are committed because the person is gripped by fear, but Socrates says: "I say that whether you call it fear or dread, it is an expectation of something bad."[18] Once more, an expectation, Socrates purports to show, is a judgment and no one goes towards that which he believes to be bad when it can be avoided. To act out of fear or dread is a measurement: "I will not pursue this path because I am afraid and instead I will run from this object." Thus being overcome by either pleasure or fear is impossible.

Akrasia has been proven impossible, or so believes Socrates. But if this is true then what does the phrase "being overcome by pleasure" denote? What is the metaphysical status of *akrasia*? According to Socrates, simply ignorance: "So this is what being overcome by pleasure is—ignorance in the highest degree, and it is this which Protagoras and Prodicus and Hippias claim to cure."[19] To be overcome by pleasure is simply to fail to measure correctly. Indeed, Socrates goes further and suggests that "To give in to oneself is nothing other than ignorance, and to control oneself is nothing other than wisdom."[20] Socrates, in a word, eliminates the phrase "being overcome by pleasure" by claiming that it does not denote a substantive thing nor causal power. It is nothing more than ignorance.

To be eliminated in a philosophical sense of this word is to have essentially no ontological status whatsoever. Eliminative materialism is a popular metaphysical position that might help to shed light on what it means for some thing to be eliminated. "Entities" that might be good candidates for elimination, as argued by some philosophers and scientists, include ghosts, souls, will, life-force, and even minds. "Entities" once eliminated are not reduced to more basic physical processes; they are not considered worthy of philosophical reflection. They are akin to square circles or *flatus vocis.*[21]

The thorough-going eliminativist holds that supernatural terms such as ghosts, spirits, souls, or God, should be simply eliminated from all philosophical discussion. Those philosophies and philosophers who employ such supernatural terms are simply cast out from philosophical debate. But such ideas are not entertained because of obstinacy on the part of the eliminativist: they are not carefully considered, rather, because they

18. Plato, *Protagoras,* 358 D, 787
19. Plato, *Protagoras,* 358 E, 787
20. Plato, *Protagoras,* 358 C, 787.
21. Literally "Empty Sound."

are semantically incoherent. Take the example of ghosts. Though there are some who call themselves "ghost-hunters," an eliminativist philosopher would have a hard time understanding what precisely such individuals are "hunting." We cannot understand what a ghost is, so argues the eliminativist, because it would seem to defy our current conceptual categories that we have for entities. Entities cannot have non-physical presences and yet cause physical disturbances. Of course forces such as gravity are able to cause physical repercussions without being material, but gravity is a law of the universe, not an entity like a ghost.[22]

Moral incontinence, then, according to Socrates, would be a name for an action that does not truly exist. It is a naïve and uneducated explanation for some behavioral phenomenon in much the same way that a ghost might be an explanation for some event that might be difficult to explain in more naturalistic terms. His account now complete, Socrates believes he has dispelled the popular myth of reason which holds that when reason is confronted by passion or fear it becomes a slave. With this popular myth debunked, Socrates now prepares the first step towards a theory of true virtue.

SOCRATES' ACCOUNT OF *AKRASIA*: 3 PROBLEMS:

Socrates' interpretation of *akrasia* is radical, but it rests on several problematic pillars. Each of these problems may, of course, be challenged from a Socratic point of view, and I will seek to provide a charitable defense of Socrates' position while examining all three problems in greater detail. We have already seen that one could argue that Socrates' "calculative framework of human action" is not innate and unavoidable as he claims. It is a narrative that is chosen. The goal of this section is now to examine some of the flaws from within the framework itself.

The first of Socrates' problem with his position has to do with an assumption that is implicit in the adoption of the framework. The assumption is that desires are evaluative in nature. Desires are infused with cognition and therefore cannot spring from some purely non-cognitive, irrational

---

22. The most prominent eliminativist is Paul Churchland. See his book, *Matter and Consciousness*. To be eliminated in a philosophical sense of this word is to have essentially no ontological status whatsoever. Such "entities" or faculties once eliminated are not reduced to more basic physical processes; they are not considered worthy of philosophical reflection. For more on Eliminativism, see Lightbody, *The Problem of Naturalism*, 60–62.

source like appetite or spirit, to use Plato's later explanation for the origin for non-rational desires in *The Republic*. There is no appetite that is not already a judgment, so Socrates claims. What's more, desires do not have any power independently of reason. There is no "overcoming" of reason in any meaningful sense of the term because desires are already infused with reason. Reason is inseparable from a specific pursuit of pleasure or from a specific avoidance of some object that produces fear in an agent. Measuring is always taking place in either situation.

Looking at the objection from another angle, Socrates assumes that desires can be extinguished through an act of sheer mental effort. If we measure correctly then presumably we cannot be overcome by passion because passion is nothing more than failing to measure accurately. Yet such a view does seem strange to the modern reader and certainly seemed strange to Socrates' contemporaries. Socrates assumes that if we are motivated to reach the Good and the Good can only be reached *via* reason then reason can also put us on the right path if we stray. Reason itself has the power to drag desire back to its rightful spot. Indeed, even if we are hedonists and therefore act only for the sake of maximizing pleasure, we remain rational hedonists and therefore are always searching for ways to maximize our pleasure over the long-run. Once more, if we measure correctly then reason can drag desire back to its due spot, which, in this case, would be maximizing our return with respect to pleasure. Such a "maximization" may entail living a relatively pain-free existence over the course of many years instead of living a pleasure-soaked existence for a very short period of time and a miserable existence for many years thereafter.

Yet Socrates' entire position rests on the question: "What is reason's rightful spot?" As Kenneth Dorter has argued, Socrates is an advocate of moral intellectualism with respect to *akrasia*. Presumably we can see through the evil of desire if our rational powers are up to the task. We can view the desire from the long-arm of reason: and make a more considered judgment.[23] This emphasis on moral intellectualism would then give the causal advantage to reason itself. It turns out that Socrates advances the opposite position to that of the common view! For where the common view holds that it is desire that drags reason about as if it were a slave, according to Socrates, it is reason that is master over desire.

If reason is master and desire a slave to reason then what role do desires, appetites, or spirit play regarding the actions or non-actions taken

23. See Dorter, "Weakness and Will in Plato's *Republic*," 1.

by a subject? Are such attributes of a person mere will-o'-the-wisps, which lack true causal efficacy? But if so, what role do they play? What is their purpose? These and other related questions lead to the second problem with Socrates' account of *akrasia*: What drives us to use reason?

To be fair, in *Protagoras*, Plato gives us a vague idea as to how reason may be used in the pursuit of virtue. Socrates hints that we might be led towards the Good by using reason correctly. Reason directs us to wisdom and wisdom remains our true goal as human beings *qua* humans. But this is only one possible way to explain human action. And besides, even if Socrates is correct, he has not revealed the causal underpinnings that are responsible for providing us with this "call to reason."

But even more problematic is what Socrates has to say about the main position on conscious action that he discusses in the dialogue, e.g., Hedonism. If when we pursue some object of pleasure we are at the same time making a measurement, then what causes us to make this measurement? What drives us to measure in the first place? The obvious answer would be the drive for pleasure itself. Now, Socrates is correct when he claims that pleasure cannot be pursued in and of itself. The pursuit of pleasure is always an indirect affair, but a cognitive affair nonetheless, as Socrates demonstrates. This claim can be proven in two ways. First, pleasure is not some abstract feeling, but appears to be qualified whenever experienced. We speak of sexual pleasure, gourmet pleasure, aesthetic pleasure, etc. All of these experiences are pleasurable, but they denote very different experiences. They are very different forms of pleasure. Pleasure is not something that is experienced *simpliciter*. It is always qualified. In addition, pleasure is something that is quantifiable, though perhaps without much precision. We can certainly compare sexual experiences that were more pleasurable than others. The same is also true for aesthetic pleasure and intellectual pleasure.

Second, when we seek pleasure, we do not seek the abstract idea itself. We seek the object that we believe will satisfy our desire for that specific pleasure. We attend the new exhibit at the art gallery, for example, because we are seeking a particular kind of pleasure. We may anticipate that we will experience some pleasure as a result of our attendance, but we cannot be certain. The same is also true for even the drug addict who seeks pleasure *via* some drug. The drug addict is not seeking pleasure *per se*, even though he might claim, rather abstractly, that he is looking for his "next hit." No, what he is looking for is that "good hit," that "cool buzz," that specific type of effect or that experience of pleasure that he knows so well. Thus, though the drug user may seem to be chasing after pleasure in the abstract, it is clear that even here the pursuit of a drug or a combination thereof, is always for the sake of some experience that has been identified as pleasurable or, alternatively, a set of experiences that overall are evaluated as pleasurable.

Continuing with this line of inquiry, the drug user and abuser, so argues Socrates, does not pursue pleasure in the abstract, but pursues his interests. We might demonstrate this by first noting that there are many different highs: one drug produces a more profound, but also very different, experience than some other. Some users will pursue one drug and others pursue some other, even though both have experienced the same type of drugs. Secondly, there is no guarantee that the drug will produce the kind nor intensity of pleasure that an addict is looking for. It may be that the potency of the drug has been watered-down or perhaps the drug is too potent and the addict overdoses. In other words, an addict must be a master micro-measurer: an addict must assess the source of the drug, the amount taken, his tolerance level, and so forth in order (a) to have the most profound and pleasurable experience possible; and (b) not to overdose.

From the above analysis, Socrates' position seems to be further cemented because all pleasure, even pleasure derived from powerful narcotics, must come from some object or circumstance that produces an experience in the agent. Reason, therefore, cannot be overcome by pleasure, for to weigh desires is to measure and, presumably, the desire for pleasure does not possess the power of measurement. Nevertheless, if reason's sole responsibility is to measure the pleasure that might be derived from some experience, then it follows that reason, even by Socrates' own analysis, is nothing more than a calculator for pleasure! It is the drive for pleasure that thrusts reason to seek some concrete object or experience. Reason may not be pulled by desire, but it is pushed to compare and evaluate objects that desire, *sans* object, presents before it. Socrates' victory of reason over desire is a pyrrhic one: one can maintain that a specific desire is always shot through with rationality, thus transmuting into an interest, but the drive to acquire some object would be beyond all measurement. Indeed there does seem to be some strong introspective evidence to suggest that this account is correct. There are times when we experience a very strong drive "to do something," to have some pleasurable experience, without having this drive attached to a clear object. When this occurs, it appears that our reason is then put into service, as it were, in order to find the appropriate object that will fulfill this inchoate need for pleasure.

The upshot of the discussion so far is this: Socrates has not explained what causes us to pursue pleasure and, as such, being overcome by pleasure, in the drive sense of the term, remains a live option. *Akrasia* is possible on a subterranean level. Socrates' view of the soul appears incoherent: desire is infused with cognition, and yet what drives us to pursue anything remains a mystery.

This leads us to the third and final problem with Socrates' position: that x amount of pleasure that can be had now is equal to x amount of pleasure in the future. More perspicuously put, Socrates assumes that pleasure in the present and future are comparable. Socrates says:

> For if someone were to say: But Socrates, the immediate pleasure is very much different from the pleasant and the painful at a later time, I would reply they are not different in any other way than by pleasure and pain for there is no other way that they could differ. Weighing is a good analogy; you put the pleasures together and the pains together, both the near and the remote, on the balance scale, and then say which of the two is more.[24]

The equation that Socrates makes above is a false one, at least empirically speaking. George Ainslie shows that human beings are built to "discount the future" (sometimes also referred to as hyperbolic discounting). Ainslie devised experiments where college students were given the option of having a lesser reward now or a great reward later (e.g., students could have $1 now or $3 three days from now).[25] Time and time again, the vast majority of college students chose to have the lesser reward now. This finding, Ainslie claims, is clearly irrational: for what investment vehicle will triple one's return in just three days! From these and other such experiments, Ainslie concludes that discounting future rewards is hard-wired into our species. What's more, Ainslie's experiments have been confirmed by other researchers and while it is possible to learn to overcome the very strong desire to discount future states of pleasure, the experiments seem to show that humans and indeed mammals in general are hard-wired to seek immediate rewards now at the expense of greater rewards later.[26]

24. Plato, *Protagoras,* 356b-c, 785.

25. See Ainslie, *Breakdown of Will,* chapter 3.

26. See Yi, et al., "Restricted Psychological Horizon in Active Methamphetamine Users."

We might of course question the validity of Ainslie's experiments by pointing out that the sums of money are simply not enough to entice us to wait three days. That is to say, our collective rationality might shine through if the rewards were greatly amplified. If, for example, we could choose to have $1,000,000 now or $3,000,000 three days from now the results of the experiment might greatly differ. Unfortunately, such an experiment would be impossible to test as it would very quickly bankrupt the industry or university that sought to put it into practice.

Ainslie's experiments, however, do seem to support Socrates' theory, at least conceptually speaking: if we simply compared our reasoning of the $1,000,000 example to our $1 example then surely we would realize that the ratios are the same: if I wait three days I will receive three times as much money than if I take the money now. Students who do not take the money are being unwise and suffering from ignorance.

And yet one can readily show that no reason is ever *self*-grounded: for it is possible that we would always take lesser rewards now given the circumstances at hand. Present and future states are never truly equal and therefore the two states are incomparable. Even here, with what appears to be an obvious choice, a "no-brainer," we may still rationally question which option is truly the better deal, all things considered. Turning to the original example, it is perfectly reasonable to ask the following series of questions: "How am I to collect $3 three days from now?" "Will I have to pick it up from my professor's office?" "But that means taking a needless trip into school as I do not attend classes that day." "Will the Professor give me the money to me at the next class? But what if he forgets?" "Will I need to remind him?" "How embarrassing will this be?" "What if he doesn't have the money on him and I have to trek back to his office while he natters on about some ridiculous theory?" Besides we might further reason, "payday is only two days away. By that time $3 will be relatively insignificant. But I am hungry now and I have no money on me. Besides, I know that the school store is having a sale on my favorite chocolate bar. If I do not take the money now I can't buy the chocolate bar, etc."

Similar considerations might also cause us to reconsider the "obvious" choice of taking $3,000,000 three days from now as opposed to $1,000,000 right now. For example, we reconsider the more "rational" choice in light of the following questions: "Will the professor honor his promise?" "What recourse do I have if he says later that he was simply joking!" "Is it possible for him to get $3,000,000?" And we might further reason: "But the

$1,000,000 is here right now." And so forth. Once more there are very good reasons to think it is better to take the lesser, but immediate, reward now, all things considered, than waiting for a greater reward, which might never materialize.

Still another way to develop this criticism of Socrates is to examine Ainslie's experiments from an Epimethean viewpoint. The Epimethean view says that a powerful desire should be fulfilled now. Return to the chocolate bar example above. Consider the following: I put off my desire to have a chocolate bar because I reason I can have three, three days from now. From a Promethean point of view, it is clearly better to wait three days—the pleasure I will receive is three times as great! From an Epimethean view, however, there is a very good possibility that the same chocolate bars will not taste as sweet—sometimes absence does in fact make the heart grow fonder, but we might also suffer a disappointment if there is too much buildup for some object. What's more, a desire that takes hold of us and is satisfied completely by one chocolate bar might be not only more pleasurable, but more memorable. And memories can be great sources of pleasure in the future. How often have we remembered some food object: ice cream, cake, pie, etc., and have thought, "this is the best pie I have ever tasted!" Moreover, we remember such paragons of excellence and compare future experiences with these paradigms and what we discover is that no matter how good these future items might be they never quite measure up to what we take to be the standard.

So what was it about that piece of cake that made it that standard for all others? Was it the cake itself? Was it the environment in which it was eaten? Perhaps. Or perhaps it was a perfect storm: just as two cold fronts might meet cancelling out each other, perhaps an experience is memorable when a very strong desire is satisfied completely. A powerful desire is matched pull for push: the pull of the desire is negated by the object it desires. And so the next time some desire washes over us and we think: "Boy I could really go for a piece of German chocolate cake right now!" perhaps it should be fulfilled without question. Never mind spoiling our appetite. Never mind our waistline. We will have more appetites and any calories ingested can be worked off. But what we do not have control over are those moments when we are in the throes of some particular desire.

Still another very strong reason to pursue proximal pleasures of lesser value over greater distal pleasures is the very real fear of death. If death is possible at any moment and tomorrow is not guaranteed, then there is a strong incentive to take what can be gotten now and to allow tomorrow to take care of itself. Certainly gratifying our basic needs now would have a survival advantage, from an evolutionary perspective, because attaining and securing the basic needs of life were exceedingly difficult prior to the advent of civilization. This, of course, does not mean that it is one's best strategy to pursue immediate pleasures over all distal pleasures of a greater value, rather it entails that if one truly wishes to maximize pleasure over the course of one's life that a mixed strategy needs to be employed. Immediate but lesser pleasures must have their place along with more valuable, distal desires. But how this balance is struck, seemingly, cannot be determined by reason for there is a tremendous pleasure in acting spontaneously on a desire.

Examining the problems with Socrates' position on *akrasia* here in the *Protagoras* reveals that Plato had an incoherent model of the soul. In the early period of Plato's writing, we encounter an agent who has rootless intentions: agents pursue interests based on reasons, but why such reasons are thought to be good is left unanswered. This problem—i.e., identifying the root of action—I shall call the *impellation problem*. It is an issue that Plato will eventually answer in a most profound and intriguing manner as will be shown. Before looking at Plato's considered answer to this most perplexing problem, it is helpful to examine the process of Plato's philosophical development regarding this issue. I therefore turn to a dialogue that bridges Plato's early and middle works in order to show how and why Plato begins to shed the vestiges of moral intellectualism.

PLATO'S SHIFT: *AKRASIA* IN THE *MENO*

In *Meno* we see a similar problem of articulating the root or engine of action. Most scholars mine the *Meno* for its epistemic discussions on innate knowledge.[27] But there is also an interesting conversation regarding motivation and action. *Meno* is thought to be Plato's last early dialogue and touches on some of the same themes as *Protagoras*. The main participants in the dialogue are Socrates, Meno, Meno's slave-boy, and Anytos, one of Socrates' three accusers from *The Apology*. The dialogue discusses several related ideas, such as the epistemic nature of virtue (that is, whether virtue

---

27. Most scholarly pieces focus on the epistemic features of the dialogue and specifically the notion of recollection. See Landry, "Recollection and the Mathematician's Method in Plato's Meno" for a typical discussion on these themes.

can be taught or is a capacity which lies dormant until awakened), the ontological nature of knowledge (that is, whether knowledge is innate or learned), and so forth.

There is one final aspect of human nature discussed in the dialogue and it is this: "Can human beings knowingly pursue bad things believing they are bad?" There is an interesting section of the dialogue where Meno raises this very possibility. In fact, Meno makes a strong case that some individuals knowingly pursue actions that will cause them untold suffering. Interestingly and perhaps for the first time in the early dialogues, Socrates appears to be at a total loss as to how to refute this claim. After some delaying tactics, Socrates draws an interesting distinction, which, in a rather peculiar way, appears very Aristotelian: Socrates draws a distinction between misery on the one hand and wretchedness on the other. The passage on the impossibility of incontinence begins on line 77c:

"Do you imply that there are some that desire bad things, and others good? Don't you think, my dear fellow, that all desire good things?"

Meno responds: "By all means."

Socrates: "Do you imply that there are some that desire bad things, and others good? Don't you think, my dear fellow, that all desire good things?"[28]

Socrates again employs the same tactic: he tries to have Meno respond that those who desire bad things do so because they believe that they are good. Eventually, Meno will accept this conclusion. However, he does put up some resistance to the idea. Responding to the earlier question above, Meno answers:

Meno: "No, I don't."

Socrates: "But some desire bad things?"

Meno: "Yes."

Socrates: "Thinking the bad things to be good, you mean, or even recognizing that they are bad, still they desire them?"

Meno: "Both, I think."

Socrates: "Do you really think my dear Meno that anyone knowing the bad things to be bad, still desires them?"

Meno: "Certainly."[29]

In an interesting move Meno then proceeds to divide the group of those who seek bad things into two: (1) there are those who are mistaken; they believe that bad things will bring them greater good when in fact they

28. Plato, *Meno*, 77c, 31.

29. Plato, *Meno*, 77c, 31–32.

won't. Socrates, as will be shown, challenges the existence of such a group and he is successful in this regard: Socrates' position on *akrasia* is upheld. Those who seek bad things only do so because they believe that bad things are really good. They are ignorant. But the second group presents significant problems for Socrates. Socrates' simple theory on *akrasia* seems ineffective with regard to explaining the behavior and motivational force behind these individuals' actions. The second group may be defined as those who are not mistaken, at least in so far as they know that what they are doing will result in them being injured.

Meno defines the two groups on line 77d: "Some thinking that the bad things benefit, some also knowing that they injure."[30] Socrates appears rather incredulous at this response. For how can anyone desire bad things knowing they are bad? How can anyone desire to knowingly injure oneself? And yet to the modern ear this does not sound very perplexing at all. All of us, I am sure, know people who deliberately do things to hurt themselves. Such individuals, the "many" might claim, "love drama." Keeping this division in mind between those individuals who do bad things out of ignorance and those who do bad things complicity, knowingly, Socrates proceeds to refute Meno's argument:

> Socrates: Do those who think that bad things benefit know that the bad things are bad?
> Meno: I don't think that at all.
> Socrates: Then it is plain that those who desire bad things are those who don't know what they are, but they desire what they thought were good whereas they really are bad; so those who do not know what they are, but think they are good, clearly desire the good. Is not that so?[31]

This is a brilliant retort on Socrates' part. Socrates' answer not only shows that the first group of Meno's pursuer of bad actions is denotatively null, but also sufficiently demolishes incontinence once again. Meno's first group of individuals denotes nothing because no one pursues bad things believing that the bad things will benefit them. Rather they think the bad things are good and therefore pursue them because they believe such things are advantageous. Socrates also undermines incontinence in another way, because an individual who desires bad things does so not because he is overcome by pleasure, but because he has measured falsely: he believes the

30. Plato, *Meno*, 77d, 32.
31. Plato, *Meno*, 77d–77e, 32.

bad things to be good when really they are not, and once again, incontinence is simply ignorance.

Socrates now turns to the second group of individuals who do bad things, namely, those who do bad things knowing such things are bad because these individuals seek to injure themselves. Socrates' solution to this problem appears less convincing. In fact, it appears, at least on the surface, that Socrates begs the question:

> Socrates: Those who desire the bad things as you say, but yet think that bad things injure whoever gets them, know I suppose, that they themselves will be injured by them?
> Meno: They must
> Socrates: But do not these believe that those who are injured are miserable in so far as they are injured?
> Meno: They must believe that too?
> Socrates: Miserable means wretched?
> Meno: So I think
> Socrates: Well, is there anyone who wishes to be miserable and wretched?
> Meno: I think not, Socrates
> Socrates: Then nobody desires bad things, my dear Meno, nobody unless he wishes to be like that. For what is the depth of misery other than to desire bad things and to get them?
> Meno: It really seems that is the truth Socrates and no one desires what is bad.[32]

The following objection seems rather obvious: Socrates' argument goes through only because he must equate misery with wretchedness. In effect, Socrates claims that no one pursues bad things because such pursuits eventually lead to misery. Moreover, one does not pursue objects that cause misery because misery eventually leads to wretchedness and no one wants to be wretched. Such an argument though, is clearly circular: Socrates has not offered independent justification for the claim that no one wishes to be miserable and it is this claim that Meno denies. We see the nature of Socrates' *petito principi* much clearer if we express Socrates' argument in standard form:

1. Harmful acts done freely to oneself are committed out of ignorance and only ignorance.

2. No one pursues an act freely knowing that it will harm oneself.

32. Plato, *Meno*, 77e–78b 32–33.

3. A harmful act to oneself, if done freely, is committed because one does not really know that the action will produce a harmful effect. (1 and 2)

4. Free harmful acts done to oneself will only lead to misery.

5. Prolonged misery leads to wretchedness.

6. No one wants to be wretched.

7. Therefore, agents who knowingly pursue things that cause misery are unaware that the habitual pursuit of such objects will lead to wretchedness.

Therefore no one knowingly pursues miserable things.

Even if we assume all the premises to be true, there is an obvious logical leap from premise 7 to the conclusion. The argument does not prove that one knowingly pursues miserable things, but only that one does not knowingly pursue a state of wretchedness and that those who are wretched arrived at that state from ignorance.

How would Socrates respond to this objection? Simply by noting that whenever one pursues anything one always does so because one has measured that thing. Once we realize that all things are measured then it becomes apparent that the above argument is enthymematic: when one pursues miserable things one is not really aware that they are fully or completely miserable.[33] The objects or activities pursued are in fact pleasurable things, though the pleasure is fleeting and more misery and pain will accrue to the engager over the long-run. For example, even the individual who is addicted to some illegal drug takes a hit precisely because the addict experiences tremendous euphoria, if only for a few short minutes. The activity is pursued not because it is miserable in itself, but because the individual is either (a) not fully aware of the full consequences of the action (this hit will lead to another, which will lead to another, and so on) until the individual is wretched, an addict, or (b) the individual is aware of the pain that will follow (drug withdrawal and the pain associated with this process, loss of friends, family, self-respect, etc.), but mistakenly reasons that the few minutes of pleasure afforded by the drug outweigh its negative side effects.

Addiction, then, can be explained using the Socratic model because it remains possible that one may be compelled to act in a certain way after a prolonged period of time though may not have the wherewithal to truly recognize what is happening, i.e., the person is slowly becoming an addict.

---

33. An enthymematic argument is an argument with suppressed premises. It is not necessarily invalid.

Reason is not dragged away by some addiction. Rather, one does not fully realize that one's actions are compelled by something entirely other than reason.

But what of Socrates' moral intellectualism? How is it possible to have the power to renounce a pattern of addictive behavior? Speculating on how Socrates may respond, he could argue that unless one fully understands that some action will produce more misery in the long-run, then he will never be able to conquer his addiction.

What I find most interesting about premise 7 is that it opens a question that Socrates would best leave shut: "What causes one to repeatedly choose objects that will lead to misery?" In the case of addiction, for example, there appears to be a compulsion to choose actions that the individual surely realizes are not in his best interests, as such actions in the past, or in the future, may lead to further abuses of his or her body, mind, and spirit. So, again, why does such an individual choose such hurtful objects? How can the Socratic position help to explain such behavior?

We may be able to explain Socrates' rather strange position by examining the assumptions on which his argument relies. One might argue that it is possible that individuals may knowingly pursue objects that will cause them harm immediately, but that said persons do not realize the full consequences such actions will have on their states of being in the long-run. Thus, it may be possible to choose an object that will bring with it misery in the long-run and to know, also, that such an object will bring misery now, but what we do not realize, is that by choosing such objects we eventually produce a state of wretchedness from which it is impossible to escape. If we make a distinction between misery and wretchedness then Socrates' argument is that it is possible to pursue acts that will injure oneself, to commit such actions willingly and knowingly, and yet it is also possible that we are ignorant that such actions, when committed over a period of time, will cause us to become wretched. To be wretched, then, would seem to imply that one is a failure in every aspect of one's being and is beyond any form of redemption. Given this working definition, is it possible to desire wretchedness? Socrates would suggest no. And it might be very difficult to prove him wrong.

Take the concrete example of Scott Hall, a legendary wrestler who once claimed that he "thrived on misery." According to the ESPN 60 documentary "The Scott Hall Story," Scott Hall went to various rehabilitation facilities for drug and alcohol addiction.[34] At one point, his friends and family became concerned about his well-being because they felt that he was actively trying to commit suicide by overdosing on alcohol. They believed that he was trying "to drink himself to death." In trying to explain his behavior, however, Hall laughs and sneeringly states: "if they really knew me then they would know that I thrive on misery." I interpret this statement to mean that Hall is an individual in Meno's second group: Hall is knowingly and willingly acting so as to injure himself.

Drugs and alcohol addiction certainly impacted Scott Hall's relationship to his wife (*vis-a-vis* his being a husband) and his children (*vis-a-vis* his being a father). But although he clearly desires to hurt himself as some unconscious form of self-punishment, he clearly does not want to be a wretch given the way in which I defined the term above.[35] He sincerely aspires to be a good father and he does not want his children to suffer as a result of his actions. Thus, although he might very well know that he is injuring himself and only more misery will result from his actions, he clearly does not desire to be wretched. He desires to be redeemed, if only for the sake of his children.

If we compare this example with Socrates' definition of wretchedness, then the following picture of Socrates' fully developed position on *akrasia* begins to form: in *Protagoras*, Socrates suggests that objects that injure the self are chosen because one does not understand the true nature of the object. But now, in *Meno*, Socrates suggests that one may know that such objects bring about suffering, but choose them anyway because the individual is ignorant about human nature itself. The agent does not understand that his harmful actions will eventually produce a state of not only moral, but real ontological damnation. But if this is correct then Socrates' notion of *akrasia* does subtly change from the position espoused in *The Protagoras*. In *The Protagoras*, Socrates advances the position of the moral intellectualist. Through a sheer act of intellect one can reverse a potentially bad outcome for oneself by weighing the grounds for action more accurately. Here in *Meno*, however, Socrates argues that one can arrive at such a state of misery (e.g., wretchedness) where it is impossible to find a way out.

This new wrinkle in Plato's early understanding of *akrasia*, extends the "Socratic position" in new and interesting ways, but also demonstrably weakens the moral intellectualist stance: for Socrates now claims that one

---

34. ESPN 60 : "The Scott Hall Story."

35. Ibid.

does not desire to be a wretch and yet one might unknowingly pursue a course of action that would produce such a state by *knowingly* choosing objects that produce misery in the short-term. This is consistent with the Scott Hall example above. Hall pursued objects that were mixed in some sense: they produced both pleasure and misery at the same time. Certainly drugs and alcohol produce euphoric states of pleasure, but such states are also tinged with sadness: for the addict knows that he is destroying himself by indulging such appetites.

What the addict does not know is that by pursuing such fleeting states of intense pleasure he may arrive at a point where there is no way back: the individual is fully addicted and is incapable of freely choosing to pursue such objects. Pleasure seeking becomes subordinate to need fulfillment, but this is precisely what the addict did not choose! The addict chooses pleasure and certainly powerful narcotics fulfill that request in a nearly immediate and very robust way![36] But no addict, or so Socrates would claim, seeks to establish a relationship to himself such that he engages in some behavior strictly from need. The addict does not seem to understand that by pursuing the course of action he does, his pleasure would eventually diminish leaving him in the undesirable state of need, forever chasing the first initial high.[37]

Such passages suggest that a revision of Socrates' moral intellectualist position is in order. Whereas prior to the *Meno*, Socrates suggests that one chooses bad actions not because one knows such objects to be bad, but because one has failed to measure such objects properly, the claim now is that one chooses bad actions knowing they are bad, but without knowing the full ontological consequences of one's choices. What the individual is now ignorant of is how making bad choices will come to corrupt her very moral being. Given this new model, reason is still free to some extent, redemption remains a live option, but redemption increasingly becomes less likely over time. Thus, part of Socrates' moral intellectualism is preserved, but here, in *Meno*, Socrates admits that desires when fulfilled become habits that even reason cannot break. They so impair reason that one does not and cannot know the correct action to take.

This interpretation is further corroborated by Socrates' discussion on virtue with Anytos near the end of the dialogue. Socrates claims that if virtue is a form of knowledge then it is either innate or acquired, but he rejects

36. See Teresi's fascinating book, *Hijacking the Brain*, 2011.
37. See Hernandez's moving story, "Chasing the High."

both of these accounts of virtue and therefore concludes that virtue is not knowledge. He later affirms that some individuals seem to be more gifted with respect to discovering virtue, though. Socrates employs what scholars have called "the guide analogy" to help explain the basic idea. He argues that we often find individuals who appear to be more adept at leading virtuous lives than others. And while it may be impossible for such individuals to impart their knowledge of how to live well (*eu zen*) to those individuals they come into contact with, nevertheless they can serve as cynosures for such individuals. Socrates concludes the dialogue by implying that the goal should be one of finding such individuals in order to emulate them as best we can.[38]

This alteration of knowledge as virtue seems to suggest that pure reason is not enough to become good. Virtue is not something that is innately known, nor is it something that can be acquired. We need tutelage from those individuals who have been divinely inspired. The question is: "Why can't reason alone attain wisdom?" "Is reason being corrupted by some other part of the soul?" *The Meno* opens a debate within the Platonic corpus that Plato now has a difficult time resolving. For if virtue is not innate then reason is not the sole engine behind moral action. What's more, there appears to be some other entity or component of the self that is responsible for moving the soul towards some object. At this stage of Plato's inquiry into *akrasia,* it is difficult to say what this other thing might be. In any case, it is clear that reason, by itself, is no longer the sole engine of the subject and certainly can seemingly be overcome if one is not careful. A capacity for virtue must also be present in order for a subject to become good. In the next chapter, it will be shown how Plato's new notion of the soul helps to resolve the difficulties explored here.

38. Plato, *Meno*, 98a–100c.

Chapter Three

Plato's New account of *Akrasia*
A Study of *Phaedo, Symposium,* and *Republic*

AT THE END OF *Meno,* Plato becomes embroiled in a strange dilemma: he appears to argue, through the character of Socrates, that virtue is neither innate nor acquired knowledge; the virtuous are those blessed by the gods. According to Plato, children cannot be said to be either virtuous or wicked because there is no way to know what sort of choices a child will make as he matures. The notion of "potency" would certainly go a long way in resolving this dilemma: virtuous behavior could be explained, in part, as the possession of some innate trait.[1] Such a trait or traits could be likened to seeds that, when properly nurtured, sprout. The virtuous character of a person is the result of the actualization of these nascent capacities.

Plato does not take this obvious path. Instead Plato takes a radical turn. He argues that those who are virtuous are divinely inspired and continues to develop this insight in his later dialogues as will be discussed in this chapter. This chapter, then, will examine the evolution of this insight through the course of three dialogues: *Phaedo, Symposium,* and *Republic.* I will begin each analysis by discussing the general background of each dialogue before explaining how all three dialogues serve to flesh out Socrates' "divine intuition" in *The Meno.*

---

1. See Aristotle's *Nicomachean Ethics.*

PHAEDO

Phaedo is believed by most scholars to be the next dialogue Plato wrote after *The Meno.*[2] Both *Meno* and *Phaedo* are on the same subject, namely, virtue and what it means to lead a virtuous life. But in contrast to *Meno,* where that dialogue concludes in an *aporia* (literally "no road" or "dead-end"), *Phaedo* advances several theses on the subject. To provide context, *Phaedo* depicts the last hours of Socrates' life. Socrates has been convicted by the jury of Athens—brought up on charges of corrupting the youth of Athens, worshipping false gods, and sophistry—and is now in a prison cell awaiting his punishment: execution *via* self-poisoning. Socrates' execution will be a rather long and drawn out affair as Socrates will be forced to drink hemlock, a noxious and poisonous substance. It is from this depressing state of affairs, however, that an intriguing discussion on the following questions ensues. Such questions include: (1) "What does it mean to lead a philosophical life?"; (2) "What is the proper course of human life?"; and most importantly: (3) "Should one fear death?" These questions are not only topics that are both relevant and poignant, given Socrates' current predicament, but are staple queries to anyone remotely acquainted with philosophy.

For the purposes of this book, I will focus on two positions that are developed in response to these questions. The first has to do with the ethos of the true philosopher. *Ethos* is an ancient Greek word that literally means "character." It has been appropriated in English to mean "the ideal" that guides one's actions and beliefs. Philosophers, according to Socrates, are always preparing for death and therefore when death finally comes they should be cheerful at the prospect and not remorseful. As Socrates explains, the true philosopher seeks purification—he desires that he be freed from the shackles of the body. Plato writes: "The fact is that those who tackle philosophy aright are simply and solely practicing dying, practicing death, all the time, but nobody sees it."[3] This practice of death entails exercising virtue at the expense of the body, for the true philosopher, Socrates later explains, desires purification. He desires to be free from the body.

Prima facie, this view seems to be at odds with Socrates' account of reason in *Protagoras.* In *Protagoras,* it would appear that through a sheer

2. *Meno* is largely "considered to be a transitional work bridging the early and middle dialogues." See Silverman, "Plato's Middle Period Metaphysics and Epistemology."

3. Plato, *Phaedo,* 64a–64b, 556.

act of mental intuition alone, reason can find a way out from the throes of desire. This is not the position advanced in *Phaedo*, however. Even the philosopher, the one subject who is the most rational, is so beguiled by passion and bodily desire that he too seeks freedom from the mortal coil that is the body. This depiction of the relationship between body and soul demonstrates that the body has some real causal influence on our capacity to reason. Again, this thesis is diametrically opposed to the position articulated in *Protagoras*.

The above interpretation is further corroborated when one examines the passage referring to purification. For purification, as stated above, cannot be achieved in this life. Purification may only be achieved in death, in the hereafter, where the soul is free from the *soma-sema*: the body tomb. But if purification is the goal for the philosophic life then the life of the philosopher must continue after the body dies. Otherwise, as Socrates rightfully exclaims: "If all this is true, then it would surely be unreasonable that they [philosophers] should earnestly do this [practicing the philosophical ethos] and nothing else all their lives, yet when death comes they should object to what they had been so long earnestly practicing."[4]

The philosopher seeks purification from the body because it is the body and not the soul which is responsible for all evil in the world. Indeed, Socrates suggests that the body is the tomb of the soul (*soma-sema*)—the soul desires to pursue wisdom, but it cannot do this, at least not fully, because it is tethered to the body. The body weighs the soul down with its earthly appetites:

> Then from all this, said Socrates, genuine philosophers must come to some such opinion as follows, so as to make to one another statements such as these: "A sort of direct path so to speak, seems to take us to the conclusion that so long as we have the body with us in our enquiry, and our soul is mixed up with so great an evil, we shall never attain sufficiently what we desire, and that, we say, is the truth."[5]

This position represents a significant change of direction in the thinking of Plato on *akrasia. Indeed its importance cannot be overstated.* By acknowledging that the body has its own desires, its own appetites that operate independently of reason, Socrates thereby recognizes that not all appetites are infused with cognition. In *Protagoras*, if remembered, Socrates

4. Plato, *Phaedo*, 64a–64b, 556.

5. Plato, *Phaedo*, 66b–66c, 559.

transmuted desires into interests: whenever we desire some object we do not do so *ab initio:* there is always a context and always other reasons as to why we should not pursue some object or experience. Thus we pursue interests not desires.

But here, in *Phaedo*, evil is not merely ignorance: desires come from a source that is not just simply anathema to reason, but indeed wholly and completely *other* to reason. The body has its own desires that are not only contrary to the desires of the soul, but in fact can redirect the desires for wisdom that the soul innately has. Weakness of will, therefore, would seem to be a real possibility for Socrates in *Phaedo*.

The second theme of the dialogue concerns the proofs for the immortality of the soul. After Socrates describes the goals and ends and life for the true philosopher, the next step is to show that such a difficult *ethos* is attainable and permanent. Socrates must show that this ethos of denying the desires of the body will carry on after the body dies or otherwise the ethos is for nought.

Socrates advocates living an ascetic life. The philosopher should pursue truth and avoid the appetites of the body. And yet if this promulgation for asceticism is coherent, then surely the soul can change the course of the body's desires. This ability on the part of the soul to change the course of the body's desires and subsequent actions implies that the soul can causally affect the direction of the body. This obvious causal interaction between the two entities reveals a deep inconsistency in *Phaedo* and it is one that I will explore below.

In any case, most of the subsequent philosophical discussion within the dialogue concerns Socrates' rather weak proofs for the existence and immortality of a soul. I will not summarize these arguments in support of the soul's immortality here as such a task would be tangential to my project. I rather simply wish to mark yet another shift of perspective in Plato's writing when one views *Phaedo* from the perspective of the soul as presented in *Protagoras*. After presenting three arguments for the soul's existence and immortality, Socrates is confronted by Simmias. Simmias argues for a materialist reductionism: the soul is nothing more than a causally inefficacious by-product of the body. Simmias uses the example of a lyre to illustrate his position. He argues that just as the music produced by a lyre cannot exist without the physical lyre, so too, the soul cannot exist without the physical body. Moreover, just as a good song is contingent on whether the lyre is well-made, so too, a good soul is contingent on whether the body is healthy.[6]

Socrates responds to this possible alternative for the account of the soul by offering three counter-arguments. The first two arguments are, in my view, question begging and are not germane to the topic being examined here. However, one particular objection that Socrates raises to Simmias has some real bite to it and is further proof that Socrates' early phenomenological distinction regarding soul and body is forceful and *prima facie* well justified.

This objection, often referred to as the "conflict objection" in the secondary literature, holds that we have immediate, introspective proof that the soul cannot be a mere product of the body because the soul is often in opposition to the body and for one thing to oppose another indicates ontological difference. Socrates says:

> Chief of all is that if we do have some leisure, and turn away from the body to speculate on something, in our searches it [i.e., the body] is everywhere interfering, it causes confusion and disturbance, and dazzles us so that it will not let us see the truth; so in fact we see that if we are ever to know anything purely we must get rid of it, and examine the real things by the soul alone; and then, it seems, after we are dead, as the reasoning shows, not while we live, we shall possess that which we desire, lovers of that which we say we are, namely wisdom.[7]

Socrates argues that there must be two different forces at work within the same person because there is a tension between what the soul desires, namely, to know the Forms, the ideal perfect paradigms of things and what the body desires, namely, the pleasures of the flesh.[8] Now, because we experience conflicting desires, Socrates then infers that such desires must originate from two conflicting sources. This would imply that the self's desires are really the focal point of where the body and soul meet: there are desires for material wealth and so on, along with desires for truth, knowledge, etc. The upshot of the objection is this: if, as Simmias argues, the soul is nothing more than the attunement of the body, then there would be no strife or conflict between body and soul. But of course this is false: the soul is always

---

6. See Simmias' "Attunement Analogy" in *Phaedo* beginning on line 85d–86c, 584–85.

7. Plato, *Phaedo*, 66c–66d, 559.

8. See Plato's diatribe against the body from 66a–66d, 559 in *Phaedo*.

resisting the body. This indicates that the soul is fundamentally different than the body: it cannot be an "attunement."

Problems for Socrates position, however, remain. The most pressing problem concerns the relationship between soul and body. Socrates argues that the soul, in time, may be able to detach itself from the body if it has led a moral life.[9] But if this is true then it would appear that the two entities are different substances entirely. Certainly, if one can exist without the other then the two are clearly not materially dependent on each other. However, if this is the case then the following questions arise: "How does the body come to influence the soul?" "What moves and what is responsible for movement?" "Do both the body and soul move towards the same object?" "Why do the soul and body move at all?" "Is desire the secret engine that moves both entities?" These questions relate to a central problem regarding how and why the soul moves towards objects. For easy reference I will group these questions using an umbrella term. I call this term the Impellation Problem. (Hereafter IP.)

Another problem may be called the "corruption problem." Socrates claims that the soul comes to be weighed down by the body if the soul has engaged in the desires of the body for too long. But this explanation just pushes the question back a step for we may ask: "How does the soul's own desires get corrupted by having a body?" Clearly a different model of the soul from the one offered in *Protagoras* is required in order to resolve this problem. For the sake of brevity and clarity, I will call this issue the Corruption Problem. (Hereafter CP.)

I argue that the overall solution to these two problems is presented in two different works in Plato's middle period. The first step to an overall solution is presented in *Symposium*. The *Symposium* solves the problem of impellation: What moves the body/soul? It will be shown how the soul can move towards the Good while being driven to do so by something other than mere pleasure or desire. I examine this solution first as presented in *Symposium* before examining Book IV of *Republic*, where the initial solution is deepened. In *Republic*, one finds the second step to Plato's overall solution. Plato argues for a tri-partite model of the soul in Book IV of *Republic*. According to Plato, the soul is comprised of three different parts—the appetitive, the rational, and the spirited. The ontological

---

9. See 107c–115a where Socrates describes what it may be like once the body dies. These passages are often referred to as "the myth of the afterlife." For a clear introduction to the notion, see Sedley "Teleology and Myth in the *Phaedo*."

difference between soul and body, clearly and unmistakeably visible in *Phaedo*, is no longer present for the desires of the body, as it were, are present in the soul. This solution helps to solve the corruption problem as will be further explained below.

THE SYMPOSIUM

In *The Symposium*, we get a better glimpse as to how desire, *simpliciter*, forms the link that connects soul and body. The position argued for in *The Symposium* is a partial solution to the schizophrenic model of the self, and all that this entails, as put forward by Plato in *The Phaedo*. One of these problems was that of impellation: "How and why does the self move towards objects?" "Does the body move the self entirely, is it the soul, or some combination of the two?" The commonsense answer, Plato suggests, is surely that *both move the self*: the soul is moved to acquire knowledge while the body is moved to fulfill its appetites. These two goals appear to be contradictory and irreconcilable and yet it is a singular self that feels pulled in two different directions. Plato is at pains to explain the source of this conflict.

One response to resolve this tension is to claim that there is a distinction to be made between authentic desires on the one hand and inauthentic desires on the other. Thus, my desire to eat chocolate-chip ice cream, for example, is not a true desire, or at least is not a desire of the true self: the desire emanates from some inauthentic part of the self. But even if this is correct, surely I recognize that it emanates from the same self that I call "mine." To be sure, this may not be the part of myself with which I wish to acknowledge as my authentic self, but insofar as I clearly recognize that I am in a state of desiring ice cream (a first-order Frankfurt desire) while recognizing that I desire not to be in such a state because I desire to lose weight (a second-order Frankfurt desire), I am aware that currently this is the state of affairs in which I exist.[10] This realization leads to two curious and per-

10. The authentic or true self theory of freewill and action has had many, many, defenders over the years. St. Augustine, to my mind, presents one of the most robust positions. Augustine argues that we are conflicted between the desires of the body (especially sexual desire) and soul because we, as individuals, exist between the city of man and the city of God (we have earthly desires and spiritual desires). See Augustine, *On Free Choice of the Will*. Harry Frankfurt would be another philosopher who defends the authentic view or true self view from a different angle than Augustine. See Frankfurt, *The Importance of What We Care About*.

plexing questions. The first is epistemic: "How do I distinguish between authentic and inauthentic desires?"[11] Some desires for material goods, even ice cream, can be felt more strongly than even those desires we may believe are more authentic or internal as Frankfurt claims. So what justification do we have for placing a premium on second order desires?

The second question is more ontological in nature. Rather crudely put it is: "Who gives in and who stays?" "How does one desire extinguish the impetus of another?" Or, "if there is some residual energy of the drive that is defeated, how is the counter-desire able to pull this drive towards an end that it clearly does not want to pursue?" And if we continue to use this wrestling match analogy of *The Phaedo,* then where do these two adversaries meet? They seemingly cannot be in "the same ring" because one is immaterial and the other is material: How would they fight one another? The force of this objection would seem to lead to one of two alternatives: either soul is reducible to body or body to soul.

Some modern material reductionist theories of mind suggest that reducing soul (mind, consciousness, what have you) to body would entail that desires, beliefs, and so forth are dependent on the brain and therefore that they too are reducible to some physical component or system of the brain. For example, thoughts might be reducible to "information sharing" among neurons.[12] All desire then, even second-order desires or desires about desires, would be ontologically dependent on the proper working order of the brain.[13]

The other solution is to reduce body to soul. More precisely, this solution would entail reducing the appetites of the body to some part of the soul. This solution has a distinct ontological advantage. Ontologically, we give up on a substance dualism approach, therefore dissolving the old

---

11. Harry Frankfurt argues that one is truly free provided that one can effect a first-order desire from one's second-order desires. In other words, if one desires a chocolate bar (a first-order desire) but one has a second-order desire of not wanting the chocolate bar (because one desires to lose weight) then so long as one does not act on the first-order desire, one is free. One of the problems with this approach is that Frankfurt does not seem to provide a convincing argument as to why second-order desires should trump first-order desires. Unlike Augustine, who provides an ontological and spiritual ground for one's true desires, Frankfurt leaves second-order desires groundless. My approach, namely, that of self-approbation, though similar to Frankfurt's distinction between first- and second-order desires, is both more compelling and more justifiable.

12. See Kurtzweil, *How to Create a Mind: The Secret of Human Thought Revealed.*

13. This is a form of physical reductionism. For more on this form of reductionism, see my book, Lightbody, *The Problem of Naturalism,* chapter 4.

problem of how two very different attributes, which emerge from very different substances, causally interact with each other. This is the solution that Plato adopts. *The Republic* explains the composition of soul. According to Plato, the soul is comprised of three elements: appetite, reason, and honor. *The Symposium* explains that there really is no clear separation between bodily and spiritual desire. Even sex, indeed animal sex, is one notch on the continuum of love. I will now explore both of these components in more detail.

Turning now to *The Symposium* proper, we come to discover that Plato's position is foretold third hand: Socrates is not speaking for Plato, but rather relates the philosophy of Diotima, a temple priestess (who may or may not have been a real person), to his audience. It is Diotima's philosophy that Socrates adopts. *The Symposium* addresses the problem of impellation in two ways: Firstly, Socrates gives a full account of human action in regard to motivational desire. In other words, he explains why human beings act as they do. Secondly this account is not underpinned by some irrational drive a la Freud (see the Pleasure Principle or later the Death Drive) which human beings cannot get behind—human beings, under Plato's model, can understand their respective motivational desires.[14] Summarily stated here, Plato's claim is that all human beings are driven to pursue knowledge. Knowledge is the ultimate motivational desire for all humankind. Moreover, human beings are driven to seek knowledge because they seek that which is eternal. For in a world of flux and change, only the eternal knowledge of the truth can redirect the coarse, crude desires of the soul towards its final end, which is that of completion. Indeed, even so-called animal desire is really a drive towards total fulfillment. We are driven to pursue knowledge because our souls love knowledge. Love is the engine behind all human action and interaction. I will now delineate Plato's theory of action in greater detail.

The Symposium is often thought to be Socrates account of love. But this is imprecise.[15] For when we think of love we very often think of a spe-

14. For a general introduction to Freud's work, I would recommend Storr's, *Freud, A Very Short Introduction*. For a fuller treatment of Freud's account regarding the psychical energies of the mind, see Lightbody, "Can We Truly Love That which is Fleeting?" 27–28

15. Jill Gordon claims that the dialogue "indicates the importance of self-knowledge of one's inner life. Alcibiades sees his own weakness and feels genuine shame over those weaknesses; it is his contact with Socrates that helps him gain self-knowledge, and it is gained through an understanding of these inner and idiosyncratic personality traits." See Gordon, *Plato's Erotic World: From Cosmic Origins to Human Death*, 163.

cial relationship between two lovers. Certainly Socrates' account explains what this relationship entails, but it does so much more: *The Symposium* is not merely an account of love, understood as relationship or even feeling between or experienced by persons, but is an account of the love drive including what impels it and what it seeks. If Plato was merely intent on staying within the scope of love, conceived as a relationship between two persons, then he would not get to the fundamental crux of this relationship. That is to say, such an explanation would not explain the underlying drive that impels the two persons to seek such a relationship in the first place. Plato's account seeks to explain the nature, but also the very reason behind the drive itself. Human beings can understand the purpose of the drive. This fully conscious understanding of a drive again separates Plato's account of a drive from that of Freud's theory.

Socrates begins his discourse by noting that in order to be driven to acquire wisdom we must already exist in the interstice between knowledge and ignorance. For only a being that is not yet completely wise nor completely ignorant is driven to acquire knowledge. And so Socrates claims that the lover of wisdom:

> is between wisdom and ignorance as well. In fact, you see, none of the gods loves wisdom or wants to become wise—for they are wise—and no one else who is wise already loves wisdom; on the other hand, no one who is ignorant will love wisdom either or want to become wise. For what's especially difficult about being ignorant is that you are content with yourself, even though you're neither beautiful and good nor intelligent. If you don't think you need anything, of course you won't want what you don't think you need.[16]

The most interesting part of this passage is the emphasis that Socrates places on lack: he seems to claim that lack is the reason behind all human striving. We crave certain objects, such as food or wine, or we wish to engage in certain actions like sex, because we lack these objects or lack fulfilment. So too, Socrates claims, our desire for knowledge is also the result of lack—we recognize we are ignorant and seek to fill the void left by ignorance with knowledge.

This phenomenological recognition of being ignorant is the first stage in acquiring true wisdom. Already in *The Apology*, The Oracle of Delphi declared that "none was wiser than Socrates" precisely because where

16. Plato, *Symposium*, 204a, 486.

Socrates recognized he knew that he knew nothing, his Athenian inter-locutors did not—they claimed to be experts in some area of knowledge when they were really clueless.[17] We are not completely ignorant, so argues Socrates, because we recognize that we are ignorant and also recognize why we need to remedy this ignorance.

What then is the connection between the pursuit of knowledge and love? To show and explain this connection, Plato, through the character of Socrates, must first establish a relationship between love and sex. Such a connection is necessary because the desire to engage in sex would appear to be a *prima facie* desire: it is a desire *simpliciter* for sex and sex of course is often thought to be a vice engaged in by the body. Socrates begins his inves-tigation by focusing on a sex object. For this purpose he uses the example of a young man's body. There is a clear desire to have sex with the man. Feeling such desire is clearly evident, even to those who claim that there is no connection between love and sex. The next step to Socrates' argument is to show how sexual desire for a beautiful body is not a desire that is distinct: rather the desire itself becomes "stretched" forming more of a continuum along an axis of love (*eros*). The seeking of bodily pleasure *via* the seeking of beautiful bodies is a confused and mistaken way of seeking wisdom.

Socrates explains the details for the formation of this continuum further. He explains: "Those who love wisdom fall in between those two extremes. And Love is one of them, because he is in love with what is beau-tiful, and wisdom is extremely beautiful."[18] Again, Socrates is attempting to show how love might be misdirected from seeking that which is truly beautiful, namely, wisdom, and instead seeking mere copies of the beautiful e.g., beautiful bodies.

Socrates then proceeds to outline the stages of what we might call the most confused kind of love: "animal-like sex." The common assumption is that animal-like sex is heated and passionate, but craven because it is desire unrefined and to engage in it is to be in a state where we are overcome by pleasure. As such, animal-like sex would, *prima facie,* seem to be a non-rational act of lust. But, given that we, as humans, are prone to engage in such base sex acts, then it might be suggested that the soul is ruled by some drive that it cannot fully understand and which might appear alien to it. If

17. Plato, *Apology,* 21a, 507
18. Plato, *Symposium,* 204b, 487

this is the case, though, then a Freudian hypothesis rears its ugly head and the impellation problem cannot be definitively resolved.[19]

In an interesting move, Diotima shows Socrates a way out of this trap. Her strategy is to go to the original source for the drive, namely, animals. She says to Socrates: "What do you think causes love and desire Socrates? Don't you see what an awful state a wild animal is in when it wants to reproduce? First, they are sick for intercourse. . . . Human beings you'd think, would do this because they understand the reason for it; but what causes wild animals to be in such a state of love? Can you say?"[20]

What is intriguing about this passage is how Diotima challenges the position put forward in *The Protagoras*. Arguing from a moral intellectualist position, we might claim that, as human beings, we can produce reasons for the need behind "animal-like" sex. We can rationalize that sex is required because our sexuality has been socially repressed or it is an evolutionary need that has been hard-wired into our very species and so forth. But to understand sex, even animal sex, is to infuse even this basic desire with cognition.

But it is precisely this position that Socrates challenges, informed as he now is by Diotima. He raises a powerful objection, namely, that animal sex, at least for the animal, is driven by nothing more than pure instinct. Yet if this is true then one can explain the sex drive in humans in the same fashion. Reason, in other words, has nothing to do or say as to why we are "sick for intercourse." Thus, reasons proffered by humans to engage in animal sex, lose all meaning as an explanation as to why such a base desire is engaged. The impetus behind animal sex cannot then be reason. Indeed, the opposite must be the case: reason is carried forward, as it were by animal sex. The reasons given for engaging in such sexual acts, then, are not true justifications, but mere rationalizations. Reason, then, is truly dragged around by the desire for animal-like sex like a mere slave: a position that, it should be remembered, directly opposes Socrates' position in *Protagoras!*

Socrates' solution to this problem must do three things: firstly he has to explain the true rational source of sexual desire. Reason must be more than simply a calculator for desire. Secondly, Socrates' answer must explain the affective state of animal sex without reducing such an emotive state to a

---

19. To reiterate, Freud's own hypothesis would at best be a guess, at least according to Plato. If a drive is truly unconscious and yet drives or propels reason, then reason cannot understand itself—reason would be like a dog forever trying to catch its own tail.

20. Plato, *Symposium*, 207b–c, 490.

mere act of cognition. This second piece of the solution will be the trickiest to procure because Socrates must explain how the desire for completion, understood as the fulfilment of a perceived lack, is the true drive behind sex without expunging the passion associated with intercourse. Thirdly and finally, Socrates must retain the basic phenomenological insight, which says that sex is a drive—it is something that compels us—and that, as Diotima says, it is something we are "sick for."

In order to solve these three interrelated problems, Socrates turns to examining the phrase "to be sick for intercourse" more closely. Such an intense longing, one might argue, is the non-cognitive *sine qua non* of intense sexual desire. Such a disease model of sex purports to show that sexual desire is beyond our control because, obviously, if we too are sick with lust then true *enkratic* action is impossible: reason would simply remain a calculator for satisfying desires.

Socrates accepts the idea of sexual desire as an almost uncontrollable craving, but he shows that its origin is not as craven as we might think. For the individual who, at one point, only saw in someone else the fulfillment of some deeply seated need, eventually sees bodies in a new light. Plato writes in this regard: "You see the man who has been thus far guided in matters of Love, who has beheld beautiful things in the right order and correctly, is coming now to the goal of Loving: all of a sudden he will catch sight of something wonderfully beautiful in its nature; that, Socrates, is the reason for all his earlier labours."[21]

The desire to have sex with perhaps any desirable or willing partner gives way to a higher desire: a desire to love just one body, to be with one individual. This truth, Diotima evinces, holds true even for animals. She says: "For among animals the principle is the same as with us, and mortal nature seeks so far as possible to live forever and be immortal. And this is possible in one way only: by reproduction."[22] Although this "natural" state, to find one spouse, partner, or what have you, is not infused with reason per se, it is not without noble purpose. For even animals, Diotima reminds, desire to procreate in order to have their offspring live forever. From the lowest organism to the highest, all engage in sexual intercourse (if not asexual) first and foremost in order to see their offspring, now a symbol of the couples' love, live on after the couple has long died. Diotima says in this regard: "And in that way everything mortal is preserved, not

21. Plato, *Symposium,* 210e, 493.
22. Plato, *Symposium,* 207d, 490.

like the divine, by always being the same in every way, but because what is departing and aging leaves behind something new, something such as it had been. . . . By this device [namely procreation], Socrates,' she said, 'what is mortal shares in immorality, whether it is a body or anything else, while the immortal has another way.'"[23]

Human beings have the capacity to reach immortality in a direct and unfettered way. Human beings can ascend to that which is immortal, namely the Forms, and specifically for the purposes of this dialogue, the Form of Beauty, by climbing the steps of Plato's dialectic, which Socrates explains, albeit crudely here in *The Symposium*.[24] To be "sick for intercourse" is not a discrete feeling: it is merely a point on a continuum of lack. More profoundly, Plato attempts to show that we can be sick for knowledge, too.

Relying on the wisdom of Diotima, Plato explains the long arduous journey up this ladder of longing below:

> A lover who goes about this matter correctly must begin in his youth to devote himself to beautiful bodies . . . he would be foolish not to think that the beauty of all bodies is one and the same. After this he must think that the beauty of people's souls is more valuable than the beauty of their bodies so that if someone is decent in his soul, even though he is scarcely blooming in his body, our lover must be content to love and care for him and to seek to give birth to such ideas as will make young better.[25] . . . So when someone rises by these stages, through loving boys correctly, and begins to see this beauty, he has almost grasped his goal. This is what it is to go aright, or be led by another into the mystery of Love: one goes always upward for the sake of beauty.[26]

Love of material bodies eventually leads to the love of the Form beauty itself. Notice that matter and spirit are no longer anathema to each other. In

23. Plato, *Symposium*, 208b, 491.

24. Plato holds that one advances through different stages of learning as one gradually ascends out of the cave (representing ignorance) to the Sun represent the Good the very epistemic and metaphysical stanchion for knowledge and Being. These stages are: *eikasia*, which may be thought of as uninformed opinion—in the cave analogy it is likened to the world of shadows; *pistis* or informed opinion and translating this to the cave analogy would be like seeing the objects that are used to create the shadows in the cave; *dianoia*, scientific and mathematical knowledge likened to seeing Forms (Plato's universals) reflected in water, etc., and finally *noesis*, understanding the Forms of Ideals through the Forms. I explain the cave analogy in more detail in chapter four.

25. Plato, *Symposium*, 210a–210c 492, 493.

26. Plato, *Symposium*, 211c–d, 493.

fact, a love of material objects is required in order to reach the true heartfelt desire of the soul, which is to love wisdom itself.[27]

The problem of impellation is at least partially solved here in *Symposium*. The soul may learn to love wisdom, over time, by first loving bodily things. Such things are really copies of the perfect Forms that exist in the heavens. There is no unassailable division in terms of what the soul and body love. The soul is not incorrect to love material things, but it is mistaken as to why it finds such objects desirable. The soul neither understands why such objects are deserving of its desire nor why it moves towards these objects. That being said, love, as this bridge to wisdom, as it were, stems from a lack of completion, a craving, an appetite. The appetites of the body are transformed into higher drives for knowledge. Eros is a spiritualized appetite, but an appetite nonetheless and the fusion of body and spirit is now partially resolved: the appetites of both body and soul are not diametrically different. In fact, it is more accurate to say that they exist on a continuum of completion that culminates when the soul knows the Forms. The problem of impellation then dissolves as it is the same appetite, namely lack, *sans* object that impels humans to take the actions they take.

As we move forward in *The Republic*, we will see some further nuances and complications that result from Plato's new understanding as to what the soul desires and how it moves towards what it desires.

REPUBLIC BOOK IV

In book IV of *The Republic*, we get a glimpse of Plato's tripartite model of the soul. According to Plato, the soul is comprised of three parts: a rational part, an appetitive part, and a spirited part. These three parts, as we will come to discover, each have their own unique and respective goals: the appetitive part desires material things, such as food and drink, but mostly, it craves money. Interestingly, the drive for material wealth is described by Plato as an insatiable appetite and one that does not have any natural limit, whereas, in contrast, bodily appetites clearly have parameters.[28] Reason comprises another part of the soul and is introduced, at least in the beginning of the dialogue, as the faculty responsible for calculating the self's best interests. The true purpose of reason, however, is only revealed in Book VII where we come to discover that it serves as an initial guide that helps us

27. Plato, *Symposium*, 212a–c, 494.

28. Plato, *Republic*, 442a, 1073.

to ascend Plato's dialectic. Finally, we have the third realm of the soul, the spirited part which seeks honor, glory, and valor.

The book begins not with the problem of *akrasia*, but with its contrary: moderation or self-control. In the book, Plato takes an indirect path to the phenomenon of *akrasia:* he analyzes what it means to be *enkratic* or to have self-moderation first. When he feels that a standard for *enkratia* has been articulated and justified, then and only then does he proceed to compare akratic examples to this standard.

Plato begins by providing a cursory definition of moderation. He writes: "Moderation is surely a kind of order, the mastery of certain kinds of pleasures and desires. People indicate as much when they use the phrase 'self-control' and other similar phrases. I don't know just what they mean by them, but they are, so to speak, like tracks or clues that moderation has left behind in language. Isn't that so."[29] The term, "self-control," establishes both the problem to be investigated as well as the groundwork for the solution. As demonstrated in chapter one, to control something is to exercise power over that very thing. This journey to discover the meaning of self-control is cut short when Plato realizes that such a starting-point gives rise to a perplexing question that serves to obstruct the path of investigation: Paraphrasing line 430e Plato then asks: "Does it not seem absurd to talk about the exercise of control or the loss of it for that matter, if it is the same self who both exercises control over itself and loses it to itself?"[30] Plato's query does indeed seem puzzling: "How can something exercise power over itself?" For something to exercise power over itself, such a thing would need to stand outside of itself. But this is absurd, because if such a thing existed outside of itself then it would be different from itself. Perhaps even more perplexing is the following question: "How does one lose power over the self? Who or what does one lose it to?"

Plato is not unaware of these problems as evidenced by the following passage: "Yet isn't the expression 'self-control' ridiculous? The stronger self that does the controlling is the same as the weaker self that gets controlled, so that only one person is referred to in all such expressions. Of course."[31]

The above distinction between stronger and weaker self might seem strange at first glance. I would think that in most of our actions we do not experience this sense of a "stronger" or "weaker" self at all. The self, along

29. Plato, *Republic,* 430e, 1062.
30. Plato, *Republic,* 430e, 1062.
31. Plato, *Republic,* 430e, 1062.

with the actions undertaken by a self, are expressed in one smooth action where no conflict is revealed regarding the action we are taking and the action we might wish to have taken. When we are focused on working on some task, such as sealing a driveway for example, an agent has a clear understanding as to why he is performing the task. Yet such a task might also give rise to contrary desires: the agent may wish to take a break, grab a drink, rest, etc., instead of completing the task all at once. At these times it is possible that the agent discerns a clear division within the self: he or she may notice that grabbing a drink runs contrary to the desire of sealing the driveway in the shortest amount of time—a goal that he identified as desirable before he started work. He might further discern that a quick drink is really an excuse to delay work; he could continue to perform the task at hand if he really "pushed himself." These contrary desires that one has if acted upon, can either have a minimal or severely detrimental impact *vis-a-vis* the initial intention: to finish the task in the shortest time possible. In some circumstances, we might feel that we were not as resolute as we could have been, in that we did not really require rest, but rested anyway. The job was completed, but it took longer than it should have. The strong self, the self we identified as that part of us who initiated the intention to seal the driveway, wins out over that part of the self that wished to rest, but it was not a total victory.

At other times, however, we give up on the task at hand: the drink becomes a full rest and we end up calling a professional sealer to finish a task that we know we were clearly up to performing. The stronger self, the self we identified as that self that initiated the intention to seal the driveway, gives way to a different self: a self that wills to rest. It is clear that we acted *akratically* and there is some sense within us that we were weak-willed.

There are still other times where we feel we have lost all control. We are so overcome by desire that pleasure does seem to drag our rationality around as if it were a slave. For example, perhaps an individual, James, spends too much money buying new clothes. He realizes only a few hours later that he went completely "overboard." To go overboard would imply that we understand that there is a rational limit to the amount one can afford to spend on clothes. We didn't heed or perhaps did not hear the voice within us that said "this outfit is way too much, this is not wise." On these occasions we have a very strong introspective feeling that we had the power to act otherwise, knew that acting otherwise was the best decision and yet gave into temptation. Insofar as we give into temptation we also strongly feel that we "were not quite ourselves" with respect to the actions we took.

To claim that "we are not quite ourselves" when we give into these actions is revealing, or so Plato thinks. When one resists grave temptation, we normally ascribe the property of "self-mastery" to the individual. And likewise, when we give into temptation we think that we are weak-willed. There seem to be two aspects to this phenomenon of giving into temptation: one is cognitive while the other is more affective. Cognitively, we clearly understand that we are "going beyond the bounds" of good reason. We understand that giving into temptation is not the best thing to do, all things considered.

However, there is a more deeply felt, complex affective state of being. When we are tempted to pursue some object, which is not in our best interest to pursue, all things considered, we feel that there is a source of deep conflict within the self. There is a tension or pull between two very different contrary desires. Secondly, there is a sense in which we are taking an action that runs counter to our true self and we experience a "defeat," a loss of self. Plato identifies both of these affective components in the following passage:

> Nonetheless the expression is apparently trying to indicate that, in the soul of that very person, there is a better part and a worse one and that, whenever the naturally better part is in control of the worse, this is expressed by saying that the person is self-controlled or master of himself. . . . But when, on the other hand, the smaller and better part is over-powered by the larger, because of bad upbringing or bad company, this is called being self-defeated or licentious and is a reproach.[32]

To explain this better and worse part, Plato now proceeds to introduce the divisions he has used when discussing a city-state, in book three, as an analog to the soul. Plato will then overlay this analog onto the tripartite soul. Thus, according to Plato, every city-state (*polis*) is comprised of three classes of people: the philosopher type, the merchant type, and the warrior type. Some city-states, however, will be ruled by one group. In the same manner, Plato suggests that every individual is a representation of this complexion of a city state and likewise some will lean more toward one part of the soul rather than another. Plato writes in this regard: "Then if an individual has these same three parts in his soul, we will expect him to be correctly called by the same names as the city if he has the same conditions

32. Plato, *Republic*, 431a–b, 1063.

in them. Then once again we've come upon an easy question, namely, does the soul have these three parts in it or not?"[33]

From this passage, it is clear that Plato wishes to argue the following position: the disparate agendas of reason, spirit, and appetite all exist within the same soul much as one can claim that the agendas of philosophers, warriors, and merchants, though very different from one another, exist within the same city. At first glance, this likening of the rule of a soul to that of a city, may appear suspect: in a city, there are three distinct groups and each group has its own agenda. When groups are forced to live together with one another, then one can say, without a trace of incoherence, that all three groups are part of the same larger grouping, namely the city, but that each group has its own unique agenda. The problem with the metaphor, however, soon becomes apparent: the self is not a group. It is not simply a larger collection of individual things as one might call a city. And thus, the analogy, at first glance, appears to be a false one.

Can we extricate Plato from committing what appears to be the fallacy of false analogy? Take a look at the following example. When I am contemplating whether to eat a chocolate bar an hour before dinner or to hold out from eating anything altogether (because I reason that snacking between meals will be detrimental to my goal of losing weight) I still believe that both of these desires are mine. I want the chocolate bar and I identify the desire as my desire. But I also want to lose weight and I equally identify this desire as mine, too. Reflecting on this example leads to the following questions: "From where does this feeling of 'mineness' come?"[34] "Is the feeling of mineness in regard to the desire for the chocolate bar as strong or as pressing as my desire to lose weight?" "How can the same subject possess contrary desires?" And finally, "If both desires are mine then how do I choose?" Do I choose to fulfill one desire over another by identifying one desire as more authentically mine? Does the intensity of attachment I have to the desire change which desire I am more attracted to? For instance, very often I intensely desire a chocolate bar, especially if I have finished exercising—an activity that is conducive to my more distal goal of losing weight—but my desire to lose weight *qua* desire is an idea that is very often less intensely felt. That is, the desire to have a chocolate bar often feels more

---

33. Plato, *Republic*, 435b, 1067.

34. Heidegger discusses the "mineness" of *Dasein* (literally "there-being") in *Being and Time*. He claims that *Dasein* is always mine, meaning that there is an intimate relationship between myself and my world.

pressing and as a result I often indulge in this desire knowing full well that in the process I compromise my desire to lose weight.

Plato's explanation for this basic phenomenological experience of feeling torn by two equally pressing desires is to claim that the "mineness" stems from different parts of the soul. Each part has its own agenda and therefore the feeling of "mineness" belongs to the part of the soul that craves the object of desire. However, this explanation does not account, ontologically speaking, for the tension that we clearly feel between the pull of these conflicting desires. For if we are to accept Plato's account then it appears that there must be a neutral part of the soul where the battle between reason and appetite (or spirit) takes place. Because if each part of the soul has its own agenda, as Plato argues, then it would be impossible to experience a conflict between choosing one agenda over another. Thus it would appear that a fourth part of soul is required so that these conflicts can be played out.

Some philosophers have labelled this fourth part "will." Will is responsible for acting as a referee of sorts for these other parts. According to some renderings of the will, the will does not seem to have its own comportment. It is simply the nascent capacity of assent.[35] According to others, however, even the will is directed; there is a natural preponderance for the will to comport itself towards those objects that are conducive to the soul's true calling.

St. Augustine, for example, argued that the soul's true calling was to follow God. Accordingly he argued for a distinction between *liberum arbitrium* on the one hand and *libertas* on the other. For Augustine, *liberum arbitrium* denotes a freedom of "raw choice." It describes the ability we all have to make a choice from the vantage point of a number of competing options. For example, if we are hungry and find ourselves at a food court, we have the option of picking from burgers, pizza, pasta, gyros, etc., to eat. We might summarize this freedom as the ability to act otherwise. We need not choose burgers; we may have pizza or even refrain from eating at all. Such a capacity presupposes that there are at least two possible choices before us and we have the freedom to choose either option.[36]

But, Augustine argues, notice what happens if we examine this freedom to act otherwise more closely. If one were to ask the question: "What causes me to be in a situation where I must make the choice between

---

35. Hume, *An Enquiry Concerning Human Understanding,* Section VIII, Part 1.

36. See Bourke's commentary in *The Essential Augustine,* 176.

burgers on the one hand and pizza on the other?" It is clear that we are being driven to act because we are hungry. But because I am being driven by
some force to choose I am not truly free: yes, I may resist this force and not
eat anything, but even here, if I choose to resist, then I must actively resist.
The drive is forcing me to comport my actions in ways in which I may not
wish to if I were not so driven. Whether I decide to eat or refrain from eating, the drive must either be satisfied or dealt with in some other fashion.

Augustine is not satisfied with the notion of will where we are free "to
choose otherwise" and proposes that we, in addition to this basic notion
of will, possess, as human beings, a somewhat different and higher grade
of freedom. This higher freedom he claims is *libertas*. In brief, Augustine
argues that to be really free, paradoxically, means that we freely choose
and love the path that we were destined to follow. We desire to follow only
one path, namely, the path that God has laid before us, and do not wish to
choose to do anything else.[37]

The notion of freely taking a path that one was already destined to
take, introduces some rather paradoxical and some might even say incon-
sistent ideas on the nature of freedom. I do not wish to enter into such
theological debates here on the nature of God, freedom, and so forth.[38]
Instead, I wish to take Augustine's higher-grade freedom, that of *libertas*,
and sever it from its theological roots. The question then, is: "Can someone
be free if he is obsessed to pursue some passion that represents to him some
essential relationship to the self?" And is a notion of will as a capacity that
exists independently of appetite, spirt, and reason required to make sense
of the question?

There are many other examples of some feeling or experience where it
appears that a fourth component of the soul is required in order to render
the experience coherent. Consider the example of acquiescence. I think it
is often the case that our will acquiesces to the cravings of a persistent desire. A common expression such as "caving" supports this notion. When a
person claims that she caved before a temptation, she is suggesting that the
ground on which she once stood has given way and she fell into her desire.
The desire overcomes her, and, at that point, she is "just along for the ride."

---

37. See Augustine, *On Free Choice of the Will*, Book III.

38. One of the issues surrounding Augustine's newly refined notion of the will or
some might say "creation" of the will, is whether one can truly be free to choose one's path
if God foreknows the path one will choose to take.

From the above considerations, it would appear that there must be a fourth aspect of the soul—a judge who is capable of weighing the demands of reason, appetite, and spirit and then making a decision. Although we still think of such pursuits as my agendas, my attitudes, and my perspectives, there are times when it seems perfectly possible to detach ourselves from such interests and make a decision from all the available evidence. Such perspectives may compete against each other, but there seems to be a fourth view which assesses the merits of each case. This, in some sense, does seem to be the case in a city, too. We think of city council, for example, as a forum to air the goals and grievances of each faction within a city.

But once again the case is, and must be, different with the soul, psyche, subjectivity, etc., and so forth. For we are claiming that there are different agendas within the same entity and not that there are competing groups within the same city or country. And so the problem is really twofold: firstly, not only different but competing agendas emerge from the same entity and this seems incoherent at first glance. Secondly, even if this picture of the soul is coherent, it might be difficult to justify in a non-Freudian way.

An apparent answer to the first question is immediately forthcoming depending on how we might define "entity." If an entity is a composite of parts then we can claim that each part has a purpose relative to the goal of the thing as a whole provided that the thing does in fact have a purpose and is not simply a heap or bundle of smaller independently existing objects. This way of explaining a thing in terms of its parts would also work for such entities as political factions. Political groups have sub-groups within them; a left-leaning party might have smaller groups that are more radical than the majority of its members. However, all these sub-groups might have a similar ideological leaning; they are against conservative parties.

Yet this model would clearly fail to explain the essence of soul; it would not do for Plato to claim that the soul is truly comprised of different parts just as a city is comprised of different factions. For it would seem that Plato wants to argue that we can control these disparate parts and that these parts are necessarily part of *us*. In other words, we would be one with each part of the soul at one and the same time and this does not seem to make any immediate sense. Thus, there would need to be some fourth part that would represent a forum of sorts; a committee that voted on the agendas of each faction in the soul.

Nevertheless, if this is the case then the soul seems either irreparably schizophrenic or this impartial fourth aspect, this "judge," is alienated from its very desires. Under the first view, the soul is schizophrenic because we seem to be prodded and pushed by agendas that are not ours: they emanate from some appetite and so forth. But we then might ask: "How do we weave such disparate and competing desires into an overall narrative?" Even if there is some judge who decides which desires to fulfill such a judge could not make decisions with a vested interest—for if he did then he would be part of the very area he judges. On the other hand, if we accept that we are in some sense the judge who makes decisions between the complainants of desire, reason, and pride then we are alienated from these very desires. Such desires cannot truly be mine.

To his credit, Plato recognizes these problems. For example, he writes: "Do we do these things [pursue objects or make choices] with the same part of ourselves, or do we do them with three different parts?"[39] Interestingly, Socrates does not spend much time in providing a response to this query. Indeed, he solves the seemingly difficult problem by simply stating, "It is obvious that the same thing will not be willing to do or undergo opposites in the same part of itself, in relation to the same thing, at the same time. So, if we ever find this happening in the soul, we'll know that we aren't dealing with one thing, but many."[40]

The above passage is further developed by Plato as will be discovered. It is important as it serves as a key to understanding how movement towards self-harmony is possible without positing an independent faculty of will that exists somehow outside of our desires and interests. What Plato needs to do in order to solve this problem of will is as follows. Firstly, he needs to show that contrary desires do not come from the same source. For if contrary desires such as a desire for truth and a desire for material wealth came from appetite then reason is clearly infected with crass bodily craving: reason is clearly infected with appetition and the ethos of the philosopher, which is that of purification as demonstrated in *The Phaedo,* would be compromised. On the other hand, such desires cannot spring from reason alone, because then the same region of the soul would be responsible for producing two contrary desires. Reason must be kept distinct from the appetitive portion of the soul lest it become infected by it. From these considerations, Plato believes, or so I hold, that he needs to show the three following conclusions: (1)that there are competing desires within the same soul; (2) that some, but not all, of these desires stem from

39. Plato, *Republic,* 436b, 1067.
40. Plato, *Republic,* 436b–c, 1067.

irrational sources; and (3) that contrary desires cannot come from the same part of the soul. Thinking that he has established the first two principles, Plato turns to focusing on establishing the third principle in Book IV.

Plato is of the belief that the first two theses follow from everyday experience. He underpins his argument with two key pieces of evidence. Firstly, it is obvious that all individuals experience inner conflict: on some occasions we feel that we are being pulled by two contrary desires simultaneously. For example, we might want to finish reading a novel, but we also want to watch our favorite television show. We can't do both at the same time (or, at least, we cannot do both well) and thus we give up one desire to fulfill another one. Secondly, Plato argues that there are times where we know that such desires are not really in our best interest and yet we indulge in these actions anyway. When an individual consistently pursues a course of action that results in more harm than good, it is commonplace to call such a propensity a vice. A minimal definition for a vice would be a course of action that is knowingly engaged in (at least to some degree of knowing) and contributes to the corruption of the soul (broadly construed which might mean that one's character is corrupt, for example). The above idea of vice is again, as noted in the preceding books of *The Republic*, accepted as the first track towards pursuing the true goal of all understanding, namely, self-harmony. The most important task of Book IV, then, is the third conclusion that Plato seeks to establish: contrary desires cannot have as their point of origin the same part of the soul.

Plato will demonstrate why two contrary desires cannot have the same ontological source. The argument he uses is referred to as the "thirsty man" or "thirst" analogy in the secondary literature.[41] Socrates introduces the argument by claiming that: "No such statement will disturb us, then, or make us believe that the same thing can be, do, or undergo opposites, at the same time, in the same respect, and in relation to the same thing."[42] This is the conclusion that Socrates seeks to prove. Below, I quote Socrates' reasons for accepting the conclusion before analyzing the argument in more considered detail.

According to Socrates, "the soul of the thirsty person, insofar as he's thirsty, doesn't wish anything else but to drink, and it wants this and is impelled towards it." Socrates' followers answer: "Clearly." Socrates then says:

41. See, Stalley, "Plato's Argument for the Division of the Reasoning and Appetitive Elements within the Soul" and Robinson, "Plato's Separation of Reason and Desire."

42. Plato, *Republic*, 436e, 1068.

"Therefore, if something draws it back when it is thirsting, wouldn't that be something different in it from whatever thirsts and drives it like a beast to drink? It can't be, we say, that the same thing, with the same part of itself, in relation to the same, at the same time, does opposite things. Now, would we assert that sometimes there are thirsty people who don't wish to drink? Certainly, it happens often to many different people."[43]

Clearly in this passage, Plato is suggesting that desires are analogous to thirst. There are two important components to Socrates' "thirst analogy." First, when we are thirsty we are compelled to find something to quench our thirst. Thirst is both a signal and engine for further action. It causes us to move towards the object of desire, which in this case is some drinkable liquid. Secondly, it is immediately understood what kind of liquids will slake our thirst. For example, suppose John has agreed to meet his friend, Bill, at Bill's house after he goes for his nightly jog. John enters Bill's house and is parched. He asks Bill for water. Bill, not having any water (because of a plumbing problem), offers John Gatorade. Barring some physiological or psychological pre-condition that prevents John from having Gatorade, John immediately understands that Gatorade will quench his thirst and takes Bill up on his offer. From this example, the purpose of Plato's analogy becomes clearer as it seems obvious that thirst usually involves three other characteristics: (1) Thirst motivates a person to move; it is sufficient in itself to cause a subject to act; (2) the subject's movement is clearly towards an object; something that exists outside the self; (3) ideally, the line drawn from the subject to object will be the shortest; when we are really thirsty we usually avail ourselves of the first liquid that can quench our thirst. Going back to John, unless there is some strong reason for John to refuse Bill's generous offer, it is very likely that he will drink the Gatorade presented. This inference seems to be implied in Plato's analysis that will follow.

Building on these three characteristics of thirst, the question that Socrates seeks to explain is this: "From where do contrary desires originate?" It is clear that there are occasions where we believe that it is not in our best interest to quench our thirst, at least not fully, when we are ill. Instead we moderate our liquid intake. Again, this example works well with Plato's analogy: clearly there are times when a desire seizes hold of us, but we also feel that constraint should be exercised with respect to satisfying the desire. Socrates uses this phenomenon to now prove the tripartite model: there are in fact different three parts to the soul and each part does in fact

43. Plato, *Republic*, ,440a–440b, 1070.

have different goals. He explains such disparate attitudes and agendas by claiming that they stem from different parts within the soul. His claim is simply that nothing exhibits two contrary agendas at one and the same time and in one and the same sense.

This argument is clearly an inductive argument in that Socrates is relying on the observation of events and properties in nature to establish his thesis. All things that move towards some object are distinct things and, so too, all things that restrict the movement of these things are distinct objects too. A dog tethered to some tree, for example, is very different from the tether that holds him fast to the tree. So too, Socrates implies, the force (thirst) that drives us to seek some object (liquid) is very different from the counter-compulsion if it is present (illness) which causes us to wait or give us pause. Given that there are agendas within the self that run counter to each other and all counter agendas in nature are grounded on one or more distinct objects, Socrates reasons that the soul must also possess a distinct part from where these different agendas spring. He asks us to examine those moments when we feel drawn toward some source of temptation while simultaneously experiencing contrasting feelings that suggest that we should refrain from engaging in the object of desire. He then asks us to reflect on what is taking place within us and how we feel when we are experiencing the full pull of each of these desires. If we are attentive, it does feel that we are being torn apart: there is a sense in which one desire is pulling us in one direction along a track while another desire is pulling us in the opposite direction.

With all this stated, I am now in a position to cash in Socrates' thirst analogy. When we desire, whether the desire is for an object, a person, an experience, etc., we move toward the object of desire. And if we are lucky enough (or unlucky as the case may be) to feel only the tug of one desire, then we acquire the object or experience in order to satiate this desire. However, if we feel the pull of one or more desires then, all things being equal, we feel compelled to move to two or more different things. The argument is that just as one must move in two different directions when one wants two different things in order to satisfy two very different desires, so too, the origin of the very desires cannot stem from the same source.

Corresponding to the tripartite model of the soul, there are three broad types of desires: desires for knowledge, desires that stem from bodily appetites, and desires for honor. Since each of these types is projected towards very different things (each type has its own trajectory) the vectors of these desires could not have all originated from the same source. Therefore, there are three parts to the soul and each part has the agenda that Socrates' predicted they would have at the beginning of the book.

Socrates then examines a seeming counter-example to his claim: the spinning top analogy.[44] This is a rather curious example in that there are many angles from which to view the analogy. But as is often the case in Plato's works, the reader is confronted with an example appearing (in this case in Book IV) which may be interpreted satisfactorily from one perspective, but from another, higher order perspective, the analogy expands on the original interpretation such that the initial understanding of the perspective is deepened. The spinning top example is a paradigmatic example in this regard.

The objection holds that a singular thing, i.e., the spinning top, may not be moving relative to its axis and yet is clearly moving relative to its circumference: the top is both standing still and moving and thus we have an example of the same thing generating contrary actions. The spinning top is both moving and not moving: the top's axis is neither moving forward nor backward, it is standing still. But the circumference of the top is rotating. Thus, it would appear that a spinning top is a counter-example to the claim that no thing moves in two different directions at once.

Nevertheless, this seemingly recalcitrant example, so explains Socrates, is still consistent with his claim that "the same thing, with the same part of itself, in relation to the same, at the same time, cannot do opposite things" because the top's circumference ,which is moving, is not the same as the top's axis, and so they are not the same part. Thus, although the circumference of the top is moving while its axis is not, these two parts of the top are not the same. Socrates' claim remains intact.

Socrates then demonstrates that the spinning top analogy serves to further substantiate his point because the top may also be taken as a metaphor for conflict within the same self. What the top symbolizes is the existence of two contrary states of being within one and the same thing. More precisely, it shows how a part of one thing may move in one direction while another part of the same thing remains in place. The top is a perfect analogy for Plato's tripartite theory of soul because Plato now has a concrete example of how a singular, though composite thing, may move in

---

44. See Plato, *Republic*, 436c–437a 1068. For more on the top analogy, see Bobonich, *Plato's Utopia Recast*, 228–31.

two different directions at once. And what propels each distinct part of the soul to move? Desire.

To be without desires, according to Plato, would be equivalent to a car moving without a working engine; certainly it is possible for a car to move in this way, but we would not call it self-propelled: the car may be towed, pushed, etc. Desires are the cause of self-propulsion and all desires seek absolute fulfillment.

Given this basic answer to the question of impellation, we are now inching closer to answering the corruption problem, i.e., "How are self-deleterious desires generated?"

If we look closely at the above questions, it becomes clear that Socrates attempts to explain the loss of self-moderation in an analogous manner to movement. In other words, Socrates explains such concepts in terms of why and how we move towards some object of desire. As Socrates explains,

> *Socrates:* Now, would we assert that sometimes there are thirsty people who don't wish to drink?
> Certainly, it happens often to many people.
> *Socrates:* What then should one say about them? Isn't it that there is something in their soul, bidding them to drink, and something different, forbidding them to do so, that overrules the thing that bids?
> I think so.
> *Socrates:* Doesn't that which forbids in such cases come into play— if it comes into play at all—as a result of rational calculation, while what drives and drags them to drink is a result of feelings and diseases?[45]

From this passage, it is clear that Socrates has not given up the "calculator model" of rationality, but he has modified it, deepened it. Plato writes: "We'll call the part of the soul with which it calculates the rational part and the part with which it lusts, hungers, thirsts, and gets excited by other appetites the irrational appetitive part, companion of certain indulgences and pleasures."[46]

Returning to the spinning top analogy, we might claim that thirst is analogous to the movement of the top relative to its circumference. The circumference of the top is analogous to the appetitive part of the soul. To be thirsty is to be compelled to move in the direction of drink. But on

45. Plato, *Republic*, 439c–d, 1071.
46. Plato, *Republic*, 439d, 1071.

occasion, we understand when we must rein in this desire. Reason "over-rules the thing that bids," as Plato writes. In an analogous manner, the force applied to the top's axis produces enough angular momentum such that the top will remain in place and not move forward. Plato wants to claim that the appetitive desire remains even as the top remains spinning, but it does not move towards the object of its desire because it is kept in place by reason. Reason is analogous, in this case, to the axis of the top.

What is perhaps most interesting about this analogy is how we might apply it to more contemporary views of *akrasia*. We might claim that reason keeps desire in check provided that it is capable of exerting its own force on desire. Just as a top has the most angular momentum when it is first released, we might claim that reason has the most strength when it resolves to combat a desire from when the desire first emerges in the mind of some person. Gradually, however, the strength of reasoning diminishes and the desire moves the entire top, in this case the person, forward. Because the middle part of the top is wider than either the handle of the top or its base, the top is susceptible to the torque from another force, namely, gravity. This in turn causes the top to precess or to lurch forward at an angle. With the combination of friction and torque, the top eventually loses angular momentum and launches forward.

Of course, Plato would be unaware as to the forces that are at work on a top. It is only until we are in the possession of Newton's laws of rotation that we get a glimpse as to why the top works at all. Be that as it may, the idea that reason eventually "peters out" resonates with us. Certainly the idea of a top losing momentum, and then wobbling, was well-known to the ancient Greeks. When we resist a strong temptation there is a sense that the resistance from purely rational grounds is at its strongest at the first sign of the desire. However, as we actively and directly resist the temptation head-on, as it were, the desire gets stronger until eventually we are overcome by it and we move towards the object of desire. The resistant force supplied by reason is no longer able to keep such desires from simply spinning endlessly in a circle. Indeed they are now complicit with desire: while it is appetitive desire that causes the top to move forward, it is reason that causes the top to steer in a determined direction towards the object desired.

Thus far, I examined Plato's account of impellation from only two van-tage points: that of reason and appetite. However, the soul is directed by a third engine: honor. What evidence does Plato present in order to prove that such a part exists? Plato responds to this query by recounting, through the mouth of Socrates, the tale of Leontius. The tale purports to show that neither reason nor appetite denote all of the parts of the soul, in that other forces are at work in preventing appetite from engaging in a clear vice. Leontius is an individual who cannot help but look upon corpses. As Plato explains the story:

> He, Leontius, struggled with himself and covered his face, but finally overpowered by the appetite, he pushed with his eyes wide open and rushed towards the corpses saying, "Look for yourselves, you evil wretches, take your fill of the beautiful sight!" I've heard that story myself. It certainly proves that anger sometimes makes way against the appetites as one thing against another.[47]

The rational part of Leonitus' soul knows that his desire to look upon such bodies is wrong. It is simply the appetite of what one might call "morbid curiosity" that compels him to look upon corpses. He realizes that looking upon such dead bodies is immoral and yet he cannot stop himself from looking upon them. This predilection for looking upon dead bodies is a rather curious "appetite." It does not present itself like other appetites, such as food, drink, or sex, in that with these appetites there is a conscious propulsion towards some object. When such appetites are experienced, there is at least some part of us that wants to fulfill the appetite and we are conscious that we wish to fulfill the desire. The appetite is understandable, indeed natural. We fully understand the desire we have. But for Leontius, he is disgusted with himself for looking upon such bodies. There is no conscious part of him that wishes to direct his eyes to the corpses. Why then does he do it?

The "Leontius condition" is still very much with us today, although it may manifest itself in less obvious forms. We need only observe drivers on a highway slow down and "rubber neck" in order to look at an accident. What do such drivers hope to see? Are they hoping to see a body being carried off in an ambulance? In any case, understandably, Leontius is gravely distressed by such a latent and persistent and rather ghoulish desire. He wishes to resist his appetite and so attempts to enlist a third part of the soul, namely, spirit to assist his reason, which tells him not to look. Plato writes in this regard:

> Besides, don't we often notice in other cases that when appetite forces someone contrary to rational calculation, he reproaches

47. Plato, *Republic*, 439e–440b, 1071.

himself and gets angry with that in him that's doing the forcing, so that of the two factions that are fighting a civil war, so to speak, spirit allies itself with reason? But I don't think you can say that you've ever seen spirit, either in yourself or anyone else, ally itself with an appetite to do what reason has decided must not be done.[48]

Plato's analysis of this story leads him to a curious remark in regard to the nature of the spirited part of the soul. He writes: "The position of the spirited part seems to be the opposite of what we thought before. Then we thought of it as something appetitive, but now we say that it is far from being that, for in the civil war in the soul it aligns itself far more with the rational part."[49]

Plato's explanation does seem to ring true for those of us who have ever battled with temptation. Sometimes we need to invoke our pride in order to combat some unwanted temptation that we find disgraceful. It is often the case that addicts, for example, need to have their self-esteem built up in order to re-establish some bulwark of restraint.[50] Evagrius, the great desert Christian father, as seen in chapter one, clearly understood the importance of employing spirit when resisting a temptation of the flesh.

What Plato takes from the above analysis is the following key point: self-moderation is a kind of harmony. The word, harmony is derived from two Greek words *harmonia* (ἁρμονία), meaning concordant or mutual agreement, and *harmoza* (ἁρμόζω), meaning to join together. Harmonies are comprised of three notes forming chords. Moreover, musical harmonies often involve chord progression or, in other words, there is an arc to a harmony or high point that the harmony eventually reaches in a song. By analogy, to be moderate involves understanding the agendas of each part, (notice again there are three parts of the soul, just as there are three notes to a chord) and then putting each agenda to work for the sake of a greater purpose. Plato counsels that reason and spirit must govern the appetitive part, which is far larger and, in most people, more powerful than the other two parts.

Such governance of the soul on the part of reason and spirit, Plato makes clear, however, does not entail that of a dictatorship, but rather a stewardship: the appetitive part has goals and desires that are innately

48. Plato, *Republic*, 440b, 1071.

49. Plato, *Republic*, 440e, 1072.

50. See Abueita, and Hassan, "Effectiveness of Expressive Therapy in Reducing Psychological Disorders."

inscribed in the human soul and therefore need to be cultivated and fulfilled so that the soul can reach its true aim, which, as viewed from the perspective of *The Symposium*, is that of completion. The problem with the appetitive part is that it has a tendency to go overboard: we end up eating and drinking too much. Indeed, this tendency to go overboard is especially noticeable with respect to material wealth. The appetite for money is more dangerous than natural appetites precisely because there is not a natural limit to the propensity to create wealth: one could always have more money and it is indeed commonsensical, though mistaken, to think that having more and more money is the solution to every problem. Plato makes this point clear in the passage below:

> And these two [spirit and reason], having been nurtured in this way, and having truly learned their own roles and been educated in them, will govern the appetitive part, which is the largest part in each person's soul and is by nature most insatiable for money. They'll watch over it to see that it isn't filled with the so-called pleasures of the body and that it doesn't become so big and strong that it no longer does its own work but attempts to enslave and rule over the classes it isn't fitted to rule, thereby overturning everyone's whole life.[51]

Plato ends the chapter by discussing the practical techniques of self-moderation. According to Plato, music is very important for soothing certain parts of the soul while the honor-loving part requires a physical form of training. Proper education in philosophy, mathematics, and other disciplines (*Dianoia*) is absolutely essential. When all these forms of training are combined then we have something like a stretched soul: a soul where the rational part has been greatly elongated and edified and now, along with spirit, is in a position to command: "And isn't it, as we were saying, a mixture of music and poetry, on the one hand, and physical training, on the other, that makes the two parts harmonious, stretching and nurturing the rational part with fine words and learning, relaxing the other part through soothing stories, and making it gentle by means of harmony and rhythm."[52]

The end result of this philosophical education is a life of self-moderation—we cannot live without spirit nor can we live without desires for material goods. But we must able to work such desires into a rational plan for the soul. This rational plan, is, of course, to live a philosophical life:

51. Plato, *Republic*, 442a, 1073.
52. Plato, *Republic*, 441e, 1073.

to practice the ethos of the true philosopher and to pursue that which we most yearn after and crave, namely, knowledge of the Forms.

Plato's remedy, as it were, for self-moderation is far from complete; for this remedy too is only a stepping stone to a more complete form of self-mastery which, in some sense, is no longer self-mastery. In fact, Plato has an interesting if perplexing way of putting what he means by the term "self-mastery." He claims that an individual who rules himself justly is his own friend, his best friend in fact. I take it that Plato is arguing that the strife and tension that once reigned within a soul no longer exists. For when we engage in shameful behavior repeatedly it is common to call such a propensity a vice and I think it is clear that vices are aspects of our character that we may loathe and even hate. Accordingly we not only think of them as some foreign part of the self, but as the enemy within with which we must do battle. This is not the case with the just man; there is no part of the just man that battles the other parts. The just man is not divided, he is not discordant; he is a perfect harmony:

> One who is just does not allow any part of himself to do the work of another part or allow the various classes within him to meddle with each other. He regulates well what is really his own and rules himself. He puts himself in order, is his own friend, and harmonizes the three parts of himself like three limiting notes in a musical scale—high, low, and middle. And having been many things he becomes entirely one, moderate, and harmonious.[53]

The other interesting part of this passage is the phraseology of Plato's which is that of limiting "notes or boundaries for each part." As long as each part understands its proper place then the soul of that individual will be just. In this way, subjugation of the appetites by reason and spirit gives way to partnership: for the appetitive part of the soul, in time, becomes a willing partner, a companion in the soul's drive for completion.[54]

The answer to the corruption problem (i.e., "How are self-deleterious desires generated?") is now solved, for it was discovered that the very question is ill-formed. Desires are not deleterious in and of themselves. The appetitive part of the soul does not corrupt the desires of reason; the desires

53. Plato, *Republic*, 443d, 1075.

54. Plato writes: "Then isn't to produce justice to establish the parts of the soul in a natural relation of control, one by another, while to produce injustice is to establish a relation of ruling and being ruled contrary to nature? Virtue seems, then, to be a kind of health, fine condition, and well-being of the soul, while vice is a disease shameful condition, and weakness." (*Republic*, 444d-e, 1076).

of reason always remain. Instead, the appetitive part dominates reason; it uses the faculty of reason to satisfy its wants. Reason acts as a subjugated state doing whatever appetition bids, but as a subjugated state it still resists. Rational desires will always remain rational and, therefore, the upshot of Socrates' thirst analogy remains intact: conflicting desires come from different parts of the same self. But, as long as desires exist in harmony with one another, guided as they are by reason, and buttressed by spirit, then the soul will be well-ruled, just, and therefore temperate.

In the next chapter, it will be shown how health, as a fine condition, is analogous to strength of will and conversely, how *akrasia* is akin to disease: when we are weak-willed we are fighting against ourselves in much the same way as when we are sick, the body displays symptoms that conflict with itself. The condition of sickness is the condition of being divided: the soul is divided against itself. We will see the nature of this division, as well as the remedy Plato proposes to heal the fissure within our soul, in the next chapter.

Chapter Four

Turning Towards and Turning Away
Plato's Double Turn in The Cave Analogy

IN THE PREVIOUS CHAPTER, I showed how the soul begins to look more like a dynamic harmony of notes rather than a thing composed of distinct parts. The actions of the just or temperate soul are like those of a harmonious song: just as chords must be used to create harmony, so too, the harmony of the soul is produced when all three parts of the soul are playing their proper roles. What's more, the objects each part chooses to pursue must be concordant with the innate desire of any individual's life: the pursuit of wisdom. Thus, the just soul is the one that is progressing towards the Good just as there is a natural harmonic progression to a song.

With this view of the soul in mind, it becomes clear that the "part analogy" that Plato employed to describe the soul in Book IV no longer quite fits. Some scholars have instead argued that the soul is more like a continuum, but this is not quite correct either.[1] I think it is more accurate to say that the soul of the just individual is more like a fluid moving ever-upward towards the Good.[2] There are three tributaries with each source expelling its own liquid (e.g., agendas) in amounts rationally distributed by reason. When all three streams come together, we have a perfect mixture conducive to producing the harmonious soul. If, on the other hand, the

---

1. See Dorter's brilliant work, *The Transformation of Plato's Republic*, 280.
2. This analogy may seem incoherent here, but the idea is fully worked out below.

liquids are not of the right ratio, then the soul is tainted by one of the other sources and it steers away from the Good.

As previously mentioned, I am not the first scholar to hold that the part analogy is a temporary explanation that will be deepened later in *Republic*. According to Kenneth Dorter, the just individual is more like a continuum rather than a thing comprised of parts.[3] However, in my view, Dorter's model of the self is not quite correct either. Dorter places far too much importance on the dialectic and not on the emotive energies responsible for completing the more underground change and re-organization of the soul. A continuum is defined "as a continuous sequence in which adjacent elements are not perceptibly different from each other but the extremes are quite distinct."[4] This is not entirely applicable to Plato's theory of knowledge. For this way of interpreting the tripartite soul implies that the desires of the individual are being pulled forever upwards to the Sun, the Good via the dialectic. "The more we attend to intelligible reality," Dorter exclaims, "the more effectively will our own rationality function within us; the more we appreciate the relative unimportance of physical things, the less power will our appetites have over us."[5] But this way of putting it suggests that it is solely the dialectic that pulls the soul from one extreme of the continuum (bodily desires) to the other extreme, namely the desire for wisdom. This is incorrect on two counts. Firstly, the end points on the continuum share a common goal: both sexual and epistemic desires crave completion. Thus the continuum analogy really does not capture the true relationship between what appear on the surface to be two radically different desires but upon closer examination have much in common.[6] Secondly, the dialectic is not the only engine responsible for the soul's upward movement. As I will show, there is a subterranean push that is equally responsible for the soul's ascension and transformation.

The dialectician interpretation of Plato holds that reason is the solitary engine behind the soul's ascension to self-mastery. In contradistinction, I will now demonstrate how the underground currents of emotive and affective drives of the soul act, along with reason, as equally significant

3. See Dorter, *The Transformation of Plato's Republic*, 280.

4. *The Oxford English Dictionary*, 10th ed., 308.

5. Dorter, "Weakness and Will in Plato's Republic," 20–21.

6. To be fair, Dorter does recognize that "for Plato the truth-seeking channel of our appetite is as primordial as the pleasure-seeking one" (*The Transformation of Plato's Republic*, 281). But if this is the case then why use the metaphor of a continuum to explain Plato's account of desire and soul?

and powerful well-springs for self-transformation. The question I wish to answer in this section then, is the following: "If Plato describes the just man as the man who is his own best friend, then from where does the process of becoming our own best friend begin?"

The best way to answer this question is to pull out a strategy from Plato's own playbook and to examine the endpoint of the journey first. Certainly it is easy to understand the termination of the process of the lover of wisdom. In Book X, Plato mentions various remedies that an individual—who has ascended the path of the cave and has looked upon the Forms via the light that shines from the Good—can employ in order to resist the appetites of the body. And certainly the dialectic is also important in terms of taking us to the higher levels of knowledge (*Dianoia*, etc.), as again Dorter shows.[7] But the question remains: "How does the initial turn towards the Sun, represented as the Good take place? What is the first step in turning away from the body?"

The key to becoming temperate, or perhaps better put, harmonious with oneself, turns on the very famous metaphor of turning itself. In Book VII, Plato puts forward his famous allegory of the cave where the notion of turning plays a pivotal role. In this story, hundreds of persons are each shackled to one another staring at a cave wall. They see shadowy figures on this wall—shadow-puppets created by a few individuals who, while carrying statues of animals, men, and other objects, cast the projections of these figures by using a fire at the back of the cave. A philosophical type of individual finds, at some point, his fetters broken, and begins to turn his head away from the figures being projected on the cave wall. He turns completely around and looks behind him to see the fire and, eventually, persons manipulating the shadows. From this moment, the facts of the allegory are subject to interpretation.[8] According to a standard line of scholarly opinion, some of the shackled individuals awaken from their shadowy slumber and are compelled, by the soul's innate nature, to seek the truth, to stand up and turn around.[9] We might infer from this line of interpretation, that, given Plato's tripartite description of the soul in Book IV, that it is the reasoning part of the soul that wakes up to the understanding that neither

7. See Dorter, *The Transformation of Plato's Republic*, chapter six.

8. There have been many profound and profoundly different interpretations of the cave analogy. For two excellent, if somewhat different interpretations of the cave analogy, see Foeglin, "Three Platonic Analogies," and White, *Plato on Knowledge and Reality*.

9. See Dorter, *The Transformation of Plato's Republic*, 205

the shadows, the objects projecting the shadows, nor even the fire itself are the true sources of knowledge for they too are all artifices. This truth awakens a thirst within the person and he begins to ask typical philosophical questions such as: What is real? What can I know? etc. He then sees a dim light streaming into the cave from outside and understands that the origin for this light must be the true source for being and knowledge. He slowly follows this trail of light upward out of the cave. He is at first blinded by the iridescent light before him because he has been living in the cave for so many years, and needs some time to adjust his eyes to the light. He sees the true ideas of things by first seeing, the Sun, an analogue of the Good, the ultimate stanchion that allows all things to be, reflected in puddles. Eventually, he is able to see the perfect paradigms of things, the Forms, and is able to gaze on the Sun that is ultimately responsible for all Ideas.[10]

The cave allegory is profoundly fertile and I cannot possibly do justice to the philosophical fecundity nor profundity of the allegory in its entirety here in this rather short paragraph. So instead, I will just focus on one aspect of the allegory, namely, this notion of "the turn": the turn by the prisoner to the fire at the back of the cave. I would like to examine this metaphor by using the following three questions as tools, which will hopefully facilitate further analysis. Thus, (1) What is it that turns? (2) How does the process of turning take place? and (3) How does this process get started?

QUESTION 1: WHAT IS IT THAT TURNS (ΣΤΡΟΦΗ)?

In *Republic*, it is the head, metaphorically speaking, that turns. In order to turn, a human head requires at least two things: first we must have the physiological ability to turn. For a human head, two sockets located at the base of the neck are required in order for us to swivel our necks from the front to the side of our bodies. Owls, on the other hand, are capable of swivelling their necks in a complete 360 degree circle because they have one socket (along with special arteries that heal very quickly when torn as a result of such violent swivelling). So the first question addresses the ontic question: What is this thing that turns? The answer is the head. The head is an analogue for reason.

10. See Plato, *Republic* Book VII 514a–516e, 1132–34.

QUESTION 2: HOW DOES THE PROCESS OF TURNING TAKE PLACE?

The second question addresses the mechanics of turning itself: What ontological capacities are required in order for a turn to take place? Again the mechanics of turning cannot be understood without understanding the thing that is turned. The dialectician line seems to imply that an innate instinct, possessed by only some prisoners, forces these same prisoners to realize that what they are seeing on the wall is false. That same insight is then molded—with the help of the dialectic—into a recognition that the fire itself is not the ultimate source of knowledge. The dialectic continues to pull us along each stage of the analogy of the divided line until, if we are lucky, we eventually see "the Forms through the Forms."

QUESTION 3: HOW DOES THIS PROCESS GET STARTED?

But what the third question addresses is the more difficult to answer for the third question asks: What initiates the process? What produces that spark of insight that forces the head to turn away from the shadows on the wall? Is it an insight into insight itself? How is insight produced from mere opinion? How does one take the first initial step from *Ekasia* to *Pistis*?

It is this process of knowledge that has occupied Plato's entire work. The character Meno, for example, best expresses the paradox and process by pressing Socrates on a similar question: "How does one become virtuous?" Meno says: "How will you look for it, Socrates when you do not know at all what it is? How will you aim to search for something you do not know at all? If you should meet with it, how will you know that this is the thing you do not know?"[11] Paraphrasing Meno, we may ask the same of knowledge: How does one seek to learn, to gain knowledge, and ascend Plato's divided line analogy, when one does not know what true knowledge is?

The very question presents a powerful disjunctive syllogism with the following troubling horns. Either the person knows what he is searching for or he does not. If the former then the individual has knowledge about the object in question, but if so, then he is not completely ignorant and therefore is not without knowledge. On the other hand, if the person knows nothing about the object then how does he begin to acquire knowledge about something he does not know? Plato's solution, at least given in the

11. See Plato, *Meno*, 80 d-e, 880.

Meno, is to demonstrate that the disjunctive syllogism is false: one knows and does not know what one is searching for—an individual is simply remembering what he once forgot.[12]

Remembering what one has forgotten is termed anamnesis (ἀνάμνησις). According to Socrates in *Phaedo*, the soul separates from the body at death. The soul then sees the perfect models for all things: Justice, Beauty, etc., before being placed inside a new body. The body causes the soul to forget these ideas: the soul becomes caught up in chasing and satisfying the cravings of the body. But it is the objects and things in the world of appearance, like beautiful bodies, for example, that remind the soul of these ideals, the Forms. One can gain further clarification in terms of what one knows by pursuing the dialectic. This answer, given as it was in chapter three, is only partial. The cave analogy, as I will show shortly, helps to flesh out this partial solution.

This solution, of course, is not without its own problems, chief of these being the assumption that the soul is immortal, that the soul and body are two distinct substances, that the Forms are real, etc. Be that as it may, I will not touch on these problem here because, regardless, the solution Socrates proposes has no work to do on the problem with which we are concerned. For the problem we are faced with is not so much a problem of knowledge, but a problem of desire. The problem of knowledge (i.e., How do we know what a standard of knowledge might look like?), by comparison, is much easier to solve for one is never completely ignorant: though Socrates professes his own ignorance with respect to the questions he raises in the early Platonic dialogues regarding the nature of piety, courage, and the like, it is clear that he knows *something* about these notions, otherwise he would not be able to raise the penetrating questions he does to those who claim to be experts in each of these areas.[13] Indeed, for Socrates to know he is ignorant, as he proclaims in *The Apology*, is paradoxical because to claim to know that one is ignorant is still to know something, namely that one is ignorant. But the question being asked here is not about the "how" of this pursuit but the "why." *Why* do we turn? *Why* pursue knowledge? What drives us to this pursuit? These are questions that cannot be immediately answered. For the epistemic question ("How does one know?") presupposes that one

12. See Gordon's illuminating article, "Dialectic, Dialogue and Transformation of Self."

13. Vlastos contends that Socrates did in fact have his own definitions about some ideas, but perhaps enjoyed seeing his interlocutors twist in the wind. See his book, *Socrates: Ironist and Moral Philosopher*.

must already have some understanding of what knowledge is in order for *the question itself* to make sense. The answer to the question is in some sense conceptually contained in the question itself. This is not so with the present question. For the desire to know may be a question that—if Nietzsche, Foucault, and in some sense Freud are right—is non-epistemic; it is a question that emerges from a non-rational drive and that, because it is itself non-rational, cannot be adequately explored in any satisfactory way. The Nietzschean turn of the nineteenth century, as Alastair MacIntyre might put it, holds that "Truth and power are thus inseparable. And what appear as projects aimed at the possession of truth are always willful in their exercise of power."[14]

I believe that we can answer this question and that indeed a partial answer to this question was already articulated in the previous chapter. The head turns towards the fire because we, as souls, desire to be complete. We experience the self as deeply furrowed entity: we have desires for knowledge, self-improvement, for leading good lives, but we are also entities that are lazy and indolent, ignorant, and subject to vice. The lesson of *The Symposium* is that wisdom allows us to feel complete: it is our one true love. All other attempts to rectify this longing are but pale imitations and substitutions. With this foundation in mind, I will now examine this question in greater detail by attempting to cash out the metaphor of the prisoner's head turning in the cave.

Why does a person turn his head? A person turns his head in order to look at something: some person or object has stimulated his attention. It could be that he is startled by some noise and turns his head to look at the object that produced it. In this case, some sensation has caught one by surprise and one turns to get a better look at what is going on. At other times, a subject will turn because she wishes to take a closer look at some object that has already caught her eye. If turning acts as the chief metaphor by which we can understand the process that allows one to commune with the Forms, then it may serve as the key to answer the question of this book, namely, "How do we go about collapsing the narratives of temptation?"

There are other factors that might cause the head to turn. Sometimes turning one's head is completely involuntary—it is more akin to a reaction—something scares, shocks, or disgusts us such that we turn away from the source of disgust. For example, while watching a horror movie, we turn away from a particularly scary or graphic scene. Or perhaps we are having

14. MacIntyre, "Genealogies and Subversions," 301.

an argument with someone and we turn away in order to show that we are no longer willing to engage her given what she has just said. Perhaps something the interlocutor has said shocks us; it is not something that was expected. Still, at other times, we turn away because we feel strongly dissatisfied or disgusted by what we are seeing or hearing. We see something that arouses our disgust and provide an immediate non-cognitive assessment of the situation in the form of a sheer bodily reaction—we turn away quickly. The question I now wish to examine is this: "Is this turn that Plato speaks of here in the cave analogy, more akin to a voluntary turning *towards* some object or an involuntary turning *away* from some object or person who disgusts or frightens?" My answer is that the only manner in which Plato can resolve the problem of *akrasia* in his own works is to argue that his is a double-turn: it is both.

According to the standard line of interpretation, the first turn that takes place is this turn towards the fire: the once-shackled cave-dweller now turns to see the source of the images projected on the cave wall. The first turn, then, is cognitive; it is a turn of conscious recognition in as much that it is reason that makes the first turn. When reason begins to awaken within an individual it is at first curious and asks: "What are these shadows on the wall? What do they really mean? For they are not real and I desire to be united with that which is real." But even here, it is unclear how the person is capable of recognizing the images as shadows. After all, the only images the cave-dweller has seen are those projected on the cave wall: there is no distinction between appearance and reality in the cave. There may be present a distinction between permanency and fleetingness, but it is only later, when the individual makes the first turn and looks upon those individuals who are responsible for manipulating the objects around the fire that make the images, that he becomes bemused for he now sees the shadows for what they are—mere illusion and childlike playthings. He does not understand the true source for such things—for even the fire is a mere construction—it too is not the source for cognition. The individual's mind is then peppered with questions such as: "Who constructed the fire and for what purpose?" and "How was the fire constructed if before there was fire there was no light?" Slowly the individual begins to perceive a second source of light streaming into the cave. He desires to discover the source of this light and begins the slow and agonizing sojourn of ascension.

One cannot over-emphasize the importance of these initial questions asked by the cave-dweller; they serve to jolt his tacit belief-system. They are much like "epistemic roto-rooters" in that their purpose is to uproot the simplistic, unquestioned, and mundane beliefs that individuals have in regard to the nature of the world, its objects, and its people. As reason within an individual begins to ask the above questions for the first time, it finds that it is at a loss as to how it might even begin to answer them. This is what Plato means when he speaks of only the head turning. For at first it is only reason that is disappointed by what it sees. It is this first initial turning that demonstrates the unsatisfactory nature that reason already perceives with the world of becoming. It yearns for something more.

Plato's notion of turning, here within the allegory of the cave, is suggestive: he suggests that the initial turn is made because of an unrequited longing—the world of becoming is forever changing, but within this said change there is something that is permanent, namely the items that repeat: the Forms. There have been many attempts to explain the nature of the Forms in the secondary literature, but I think the best way to understand them is to employ an idea by Ken Dorter: Forms are simply representations of that which repeats.[15] Reason recognizes such patterns of representation and yearns for something beyond the shadowy world of becoming. In recognizing that there must be something more than the shadows that are constantly changing, the soul instinctively understands that there lies something beyond interpretation, something beyond that which is indexed to perspective and agenda. In a word, soul yearns for the eternal for it realizes that any construction comes about from some thing that already existed. Reason quickly sees the end of such inquiry, namely, that at some point, there must be an absolute and eternal ontological and epistemological ground for such questions to emerge because it is always the same things that appear.

Moreover, and borrowing again from Dorter, there is a necessity to the world of appearance.[16] On some rare occasion new objects appear, but more often, we encounter the same types of objects again and again and again. They are continually refashioned according to the perfect paradigms that are the Forms. Now if the initial philosophical questions asked as they are by the new unfettered prisoners of cave make sense, then we are left with a rather puzzling question: "What allows such questions to make sense?" "How is it that we can ask such perfectly sensible and coherent questions and yet do not have the means to answer them?" Thus, these questions

15. Dorter, *The Transformation of Plato's Republic*, 200.
16. Ibid.

which operate on this level of the intellect—that is, "informed opinion" (*pistis*)—serve as a thorn in the mind.

Nevertheless, it is important to keep in mind that this is only the first turn. For it is also clear that there is a second turning. This turn is not a turning towards, but a turning away. It stems from a sense of disgust; it is disgust that acts as a strong impetus for the soul to climb out of the cave and into the world of light, bathed by the Sun (the Good) where it can then begin to look upon the true nature of things. Nietzsche, for one, was therefore not entirely incorrect when he claimed that Platonism was still infused with spirituality—the cognitive turn could not take place without an emotive turn, a turn towards purification.[17]

Purification, however, as Plato makes clear, is never complete nor is it fully achievable. The body will test us; it will continue to desire objects that are not in the overall best interest of the soul, though such appetites are easier to tame in the just individual than in others. This truth about the human condition is further evidence that the initial turn made by those living in the cave must stem from an emotive source. Indeed my interpretation is more helpful with respect to understanding why the desire for material things, and more specifically money, is never extinguished and yet fuels reason's pursuit of knowledge: for although desire does not turn towards the Forms, it does turn away from the world of flux and change. Raw appetite is no longer completely satisfied with the objects it once found desirable and with which it once pursued with so much relish. As a matter of fact, it is more accurate to say that appetite is disgusted with those very objects it once cherished and invested so much of its effort in pursuing. This double-turning, as I put it, shows that Plato's cave-dwellers are both inclined to turn their heads in the direction of what they yearn for, while turning away from what they once desired. Thus, turning is both a turning *towards* and a turning *away*. This thesis will be further developed below.

With respect to the first part of this turning, turning towards, the key to this process involves understanding that only some individuals are

17 See Nietzsche, *The Gay Science*, sec. 340: "The Dying Socrates." "What's more it is a truth that was understood all too well by Aristotle. As Aristotle famously wrote, 'Intellect, itself, however moves nothing but only the intellect which aims at an end is practical . . . for good action is an end, and desire aims at this. Hence choice is either desiderative reason or ratiocinative desire, and such an origin of action is a man." Aristotle, *Nicomachean Ethics*, 103–104." Also see Stampe, "The Authority of Desire." Of course, Aristotle is not interested in viewing purification as flourishing but the basic thrust remains: intellect cannot do it alone.

capable of turning. It is only those persons who are so inclined towards philosophy, those who are capable of making the turn towards the Good, those with the latent intellectual capacities to philosophize who can recognize the many questions that arise if one accepts an unquestioning acceptance of established opinion. It is they, according to Plato, who have the innate capacity to be just, temperate, strong of will. Plato's subsequent goal in Book VIII and Book IX of *Republic* is to ensure that such philosophically gifted individuals do not use their innate cognitive powers for evil. As Plato notes, those with the most innate talent for philosophy are the same individuals who may commit the greatest harm. Earlier, Plato explained in Book VI that such individuals

> with the best natures become outstandingly bad when they receive a bad upbringing? Or do you think that great injustices and pure wickedness originate in an ordinary nature rather than in a vigorous one that has been corrupted by upbringing? Or that a weak nature is ever the cause of great good or great evil. I think that the soul of the philosophic nature as we defined it will inevitably grow to possess every virtue if it happens to receive appropriate instruction, but if it is sown, planted, and grown in an in appropriate environment it will develop in quite the opposite way . . . .[18]

One of the dangers for such an individual, who has not received proper education *vis-a-vis* the attunement of his soul, is that he may attempt to pander to the "beast."[19] Plato explains the nature of the beast in Book VI. He argues that the beast is a great multitude of things; it consists of drives and tastes and competing values. It marks the tastes of the multitude. But the multi-colored tastes of the many are but a reflection of the multi-colored appetites within the appetitive part of the soul given Plato's mirror where the rule of the just state is mirrored in the rule of the just soul.[20] The individual, then, in attempting to control this beast is really attempting to gain power over himself: the beast is nothing more than the individual's own dark appetites writ large. However, to attain self-control in this way is a fool's errand: one cannot beat the bodily appetites into submission; one must use them for the sake of soul edification. As Plato shows, one must

18. Plato, *Republic*, 491d–491a, 1114.

19. See Plato, *Republic*, 493a, 1115.

20. The mirror thesis holds that the rule of the just city-state will mirror the rule of the just soul. This thesis is brought forth in Books III and IV of *Republic*.

transform them. Plato's "education" for the young initiates, who can ascend the cave, is an attempt to do just that.[21]

Why then is the beast pursued? How is it that the individual who has not been trained in the dialectic still capable of rejecting the life of a pure voluptuary? This is a deeply perplexing question to answer from the dialectician standpoint—those who argue that the dialectic is sufficient in training the subject's appetites. One might argue that the philosophical type who has not been trained as a philosopher then opts for the second best form of life: the pursuit of power. This does appear to be Plato's answer. The gifted though evil individual pursues power because he is attempting to master the public tastes and opinions of the masses; but such an attempt to control the public is also a surreptitious effort to master his own bodily cravings. All desire is channelled into a pursuit of power with the consequence that the individual is a slave to the desire to be master. But this desire is the apotheosis of the educated individual: where the philosophical type with the proper education desires to be complete, reunited with the Good, the evil individual attempts to subject everyone and every desire to his schema. Such an approach does not denote lack or a yearning to be whole, but rather a narrow and tyrannical narcissism.

Thus the answer to the question "Why does this individual pursue power and not the other appetites of the body?" can be explained by noting that the emotive undercurrents form a swell that directs all three parts of the soul. The refrain confirmed by all three parts of the soul is: the appetites of the body are not worth pursuing for they are fleeting and unsatisfactory. The individual puts all his energies into, and uses all talents of the soul (reason, honor, and appetites) to, extend his sense of self over all others. The energies do not move upward, but backwash and inflate the subject's ego extinguishing everything in its wake.

MAKING SURE WE REMAIN TURNED.

I now wish to address the second turn, namely, the turn that involves a turning away from the world of becoming in more detail. Specifically, I will examine the techniques Plato uses to ensure that the head (reason) and body (appetites) remain turned. Plato's arguments in Book VIII and Book

21. In Book VII, Plato advances his difficult pedagogy for those who have the appropriate natures to understand the Forms. He mentions that would be philosopher-kings shall receive training in music, gymnastics, mathematics, and of course, in dialectic.

IX are meant to ensure that we stay turned, or so I now argue. The basic question that needs to be answered is the one leftover from *Phaedo*, namely: "How can the philosophical type who desires to pursue wisdom succeed when, as *The Phaedo* clearly demonstrates, he is very much shackled to the body?"

To succeed in this new found quest—that of the philosophical ethos—Plato recommends a bodily training regime. For example, he suggests that those individuals so inclined to pursue philosophy should be trained in music. Indeed, Plato stresses that a philosophical individual should only play string instruments, such as harps, because one can pick out each chord—the harmony is fixed.[22] Whereas wind instruments involve a myriad of tones and, by analogy, when such instruments are played they arouse darker parts of the soul (the appetitive part of the soul is a beast consisting of many heads).[23] Again, what the individual says to himself before he goes to bed is also important. Plato counsels that one should nourish one's mind on arguments before nodding off and "to neither starve nor feast one's appetites," etc.[24]

These actions are practices that help to establish virtuous habits. However, the following should be clear: when one practices such activities, one has already firmly established the belief that the road to wisdom, the road to the Forms, is a worthwhile goal. One has established that virtue is to be pursued above pleasure. Desire for material goods has been severely curtailed. In my parlance, one has already turned towards *and* turned away. But what if one, much like Philebus, begins to question the very pursuit of wisdom anew?[25] What if as one is about to ascend to the cave entrance (where his eyes are pained by the sudden bright light that he now sees), he does not move upward, but wishes to return to the dark, yet familiar, cave? How does Plato convince us to turn away from temptation, whether in the form of material bodies or incorporeal power? How does Plato convince us to disperse the clouds of alternative narratives?

---

22. See Plato, *Republic* 397–403, 1034–38.

23. See Plato, *Republic* 411a-b (1047) and 561a-c, 1171–72.

24. See Plato, *Republic*, 571d–572e, 1180–81.

25. Philebus is said to have argued that "what is good for all creatures is to enjoy themselves, to be pleased and delighted and whatever else goes together with that kind of thing." Philebus does not defend this argument in the dialogue *Philebus* perhaps because he did not see a reason too. Indeed, it appears that he wanders off. See Plato, *Philebus*, 11b-c, 398–456.

The arguments Plato puts forward in Book IX of *Republic* are meant to justify the road to wisdom. These arguments, or so I argue, are intended to remind the philosophical-type to stay the course and not be tempted to pursue the other agendas or narratives of the soul. One of the more interesting arguments in this regard is found in Book IX. I shall call the argument, the "Best Mode of Life Argument."[26] This argument suggests that only the philosopher type can judge which form of life is the best. Plato lays out his case by assuming that there are three basic forms of life: the appetitive, the spirited, and the rational, with each form of life obviously denoting a corresponding part of the soul. It is obvious, or so Plato thinks, that each representative of his respective mode of living thinks that he is living the best form of life when he begins to compare his mode to that of others. Thus, Plato concedes that it is impossible to use a standard metric by which to measure objectively each form of life.

Yet Plato can further convince the philosopher type as to why a life of inquiry is to be preferred over the others. For the philosopher type it is appetite, the pursuit of pleasure, that presents the largest hurdle *vis-a-vis* pursuing the life of wisdom. But if this is the case, then it makes sense to examine all forms of life according to one standard: that of pleasure. The question then becomes: "What form of life allows for the most pleasure in terms of quantity, the best pleasure in terms of quality, and the most satisfying pleasure in terms of longevity and purity?" Putting all these questions together we have: "Which form of life allows us to pursue pleasure with these three conditions in mind?"

According to Plato, even if we measure each form of life in terms of pleasure, clearly the philosophical type wins out. This is proven in two ways. First, only the philosophical type has experience with all three forms of living. Philosophers have experienced bodily pleasure, they have competed in games of contest and skill when they were younger and so know what it means to win and lose, to receive accolades for one's physical prowess, and so forth. Now since the philosophical type chooses knowledge over these other forms of living, then the philosophical mode of life must be the best because it is chosen by the only person capable of judging all forms—the person of wisdom. Thus, even according to the hedonist's own metric, the philosophic life is the best.

At first glance, the argument may appear question begging: the philosophical type of life is the best because the philosopher deems it to be the

---

26. See Plato, *Republic,* 580d–583a, 1188–90.

best, end of story. However, neither the pleasure seeking individual nor the warrior type can adequately respond to the philosopher type for they have not experienced what he has experienced. If one is unacquainted with the philosophical type of life then one simply has to trust the philosopher.

But one could press the objection further. One could argue that some philosophers may give up on the road to wisdom and "regress" to hedonism. Is the philosophical type of life justified ultimately on some kind of philosophical poll?

From the above discussion, it is clear that there are some logical difficulties with the argument. So, what then is the chief purpose of the argument? Why does Plato make it? Given my thesis, I think it is clear that the argument is meant to serve as a reminder to the philosophical type. And just what is this reminder? Stay the course! Philosophical types who may yet be tempted by different iterations of hedonism or honor-seeking lifestyles as they ascend out of the cave should be reminded, so Plato holds, that those paths were trodden, they were tried, they were tested, and they were lived—and they were all deemed unsatisfactory.

Second, the pursuit of wisdom as a means of attaining pleasure is longer lasting than the methods pursued by the self-indulgent or the vainglorious. The pleasure derived from appetites is not long-lasting nor is it of a very high quality when compared to the life of wisdom. No matter how delicious a piece of Devil's Chocolate cake might be, it pales in comparison to the delight one experiences when one reads the poetry of e. e. cummings.[27] Moreover, many of the appetites of the body are mixed— we feel both pleasure and guilt in pursuing them. They are impure, unlike the pursuits of knowledge.

The pleasures derived from pursuing honor may be long-lasting provided that one always wins whatever contest one enters. The road, however, to such victory is long and arduous and there is not much pleasure in the pursuit itself. In addition, such a mode has a natural shelf-life; such pursuits are best suited for the young. As one ages, a warrior-like individual can certainly continue to compete in other ventures, but more likely than not, the individual competes within the realm of money-making. It is for this reason that Plato argues that honor-loving eventually leads to money-loving

---

27. My favourite e. e. cummings poem is: "Somewhere I have never Travelled Gladly Beyond."

and the love of money is at best only a means to an end; it cannot be an end in itself. It will not lead to a sense of completion.[28]

None of this is the case for the philosopher type. With the philosophical type the pursuit of wisdom pays "pleasure-dividends" almost immediately—one takes delight in the fact that knowledge is being acquired. Likewise, the pursuit of wisdom itself allows for the most "pleasure units": knowledge gains interest as one continues to pursue wisdom—one is never left with nothing, as it were, as is the case with appetite. Furthermore, one's goal is not to become the smartest person in the world. The proper pursuit of wisdom is not a contest. The pressure experienced by the vainglorious to always be the best, to always receive the most honors, the most applause, is simply not present for the philosophical type because his pleasure does not stem from an external source: pleasure is derived from reading, thinking, philosophizing. The philosopher's pleasure does not depend on a game, an audience or some other artificial construct as is the case with the vainglorious. The philosopher's pleasure is self-sufficient.

Finally, the love of wisdom is the purest form of pleasure—the acquiring of knowledge is not a mixed experience as is the case with appetite. We never experience a sense of lack when we take a rest from pursuing knowledge. Indeed, such a "break" often leads to further reflection on what we have just learned and, of course, further analysis. Again, this is not the case with appetite. When an appetite is satisfied we feel a loss. This experience is most unlike the pursuit of knowledge.

The third argument Plato uses to justify his position is, it seems to me, another reminder to the philosophical type to stay the course. This argument, too, is based on the assumption that pleasure is the ultimate ground of action. Plato then argues from this assumption that our subjective experience of pleasure may be mistaken. I will call this the "mistaken-pleasure argument."

Although we believe that pleasure is true or real according to the person who experiences it, Plato shows that we may be subjectively incorrect with regard to what we are experiencing. If this is accurate, then there is an objective standpoint for true pleasure. Plato then concludes that only the philosopher-type has access to this true pleasure and therefore is the only type capable of judging which source of pleasure is the purest.[29]

28. See Plato, *The Republic*, Book VIII 550d-e, 1162.
29. See Plato, *The Republic*, 583a–588a, 1190–96.

To be sure this appears to be a strange argument on the surface: "How can one determine an objective standard to pleasure?" Plato begins his argument by showing that we sometimes mistake the absence of pain for the feeling of pleasure. For example, when one is sick and then begins to recover, he thinks he is experiencing pleasure, but really he is only feeling the absence of illness. Such a state of being, namely the absence of pain, or alternatively "not being sick," is certainly a lower form of pleasure: there is a difference between being of good health (i.e., not ill) and being of good health and satisfying some desire.[30] If Plato is correct about the fact that we can be mistaken when it comes to what we are feeling, then the following questions seem legitimate to ask: (1) Can we make sense of grading pleasure? (2) What form of life received the highest grade?

To answer the first question Plato proceeds to perform a phenomenological analysis of pleasure. He asks us to think about when we, as individuals, experience the most pleasure. He argues that a pleasure is more pleasurable when it is pure: when there is not an experience of lack, when the desire has been satisfied. With pleasures of the body and of honor, there is a sense of incompletion with the former and a sense of loss with the latter. When we satisfy an appetite such as hunger, for example, we feel satiated, but we know that in a few short hours we will be hungry again.[31] The object, at best, can only satisfy, and only for a short period of time, a superficial craving—it has no power to quench our real thirst.

The upshot of the above analysis is this: Living a life where we simply strive to satisfy the appetites of the body is not a fully satisfactory life. A voluptuary cannot claim to live a life worth living, even by his own account, because he has missed out on those pleasures that are the most satisfactory and allow for full completion, namely the pleasures that may be derived from a life dedicated to the pursuit of knowledge.

Before looking at the case of the vainglorious, it is important to examine a counter-example. While it is true that material objects cannot satisfy our desire to feel complete or whole, surely there is one experience that

30. Plato, *The Republic, The Complete Works of Plato*, 583c-d, 1191.

31. Such reflection reminds me of an old Jerry Seinfeld bit regarding the ruination of an appetite. He proclaims that one cannot ruin or spoil one's appetite, as we might say a child does by snacking before supper, because we are never without appetite. If we wait a few hours we will be hungry again. Of course, when a parent says, "Don't snack, you will ruin your appetite!" what she means is that you only have one opportunity to have dinner, and if you are not hungry now, you will be hungry later but you won't have an opportunity to eat.

dissolves our sense of subject and object. This experience is of course the orgasm. The orgasm seems to be the purest form of bodily pleasure in that many other pleasures are mixed: we may derive pleasure from eating, but we may also feel guilty, too. At the precise moment of orgasm, however, this is not possible. There is no longer a separation between ourselves and the object of desire. We are one with the satiation of the drive.

Yet, again, Plato would point to the disappointment with the life of a Lothario or Don Juan. An orgasm is fleeting, indeed it may be the most intense, yet most fleeting pleasure a human can experience. Certainly such a promiscuous lifestyle will eventually give way to regret: the Lothario has missed out, we might say, if he has only had sex but has never made love or been in love. The overall life of such an individual will be spiked with intense pleasure, but overall there will be profound disappointment. Again, the philosophical type of life is to be preferred.

Those who pursue honor and glory pursue objects that are inherently fleeting because they are infused with expiration dates in a double sense of the term. Such a life must once again rest on a lower rung of the ladder of pleasure. Firstly, honors and accolades only demonstrate that one is the best at some competition now, not necessarily next year, and certainly not for all eternity. Secondly, there is an expiration date on athletic performance— what one is capable of doing in the Olympic Games or on the battlefield at twenty, is very different from what one can do when one is fifty. Whatever pleasure is derived from being a victor, a winner, does not last. Thus, one who pursues the pleasure of victory is setting himself up for a fall: eventually a contestant will be stronger and faster than the champion. And this anxiety-producing thought—namely that "my time will come," "I too will be knocked off the podium"—must infuse a life, over the long-run, with dread not joy.

These arguments serve as rational reminders to the philosophical type to stay the course. Again and again Plato reminds this type not to be lured by temporary pleasures of either the material or honorable seeking drives. These reflections serve as effective prophylactics against the temptation to pursue either of these forms of life. Such arguments have teeth as it were, because as Plato has shown in *Symposium*, we are driven to pursue that which completes us, namely knowledge.

TURNING INTO (AND TO) OUR BEST FRIEND

To rule justly is to establish a harmonious relationship between all parts of the self. It is to become one's best friend. If one part rules the other in a tyrannical fashion, even if the tyrant be reason itself, then the individual is not well-ruled. The constitution of the individual's soul is not just. Plato would surely not believe that Spock from *Star Trek* is the model of the enlightened philosopher. Spock rules with reason, but his reason is more properly thought of as *Dianoia*—logic, science, etc. He has still not reached the lofty goal of *Noesis* precisely because he views all reason as merely instrumental or tool-like. In contrast, the goal, for Plato, is to ascend the analogy of the line: to know the Forms by using the ladder of the dialectic. But one is still attached to a body and therefore, one must use the body to ascend each rung of the ladder. Pure, disembodied reason, whatever this may mean, cannot do the work alone.

This interpretation is further corroborated by looking at section 518c of the *Republic*. Towards the end of the cave analogy, Socrates remarks that "the power to learn is in everyone's soul and that the instrument with which each learns is like an eye that cannot be turned around from darkness to light without turning the whole body."[32] To turn the eye towards the sun and away from darkness requires a complete turning, a complete 180 degree shift. Education is the instrument that Plato refers to above that is responsible for said turning. But true education cannot be had unless the student is not just able to learn, but is willing to learn. A thirst for knowledge has to be cultivated in the individual before he submits to being educated. Such a thirst, though, depends on our recognition that we are ignorant. Such recognition, though, at first, is felt to be shameful and embarrassing.[33] But it is these negative emotions that provide the push the individual needs to reach for the tow-line of the dialectic and to ascend the cave. In so doing, the individual's soul is reoriented, fully turned towards the Good.

As we discovered, the soul is much like a river that is sourced by three tributaries. All three tributaries must come together in order for the soul to pursue its goal. We can now add to this metaphor and claim that the soul is being carried forward on a water ladder. A water ladder is a method of irrigation where water is carried upward on a long trough by wheel, chain,

32. Plato, *Republic*, 518c, 1136.

33. See Plato, *The Euthyphro* for an example where Euthyphro, a person who claims to know about justice, is thoroughly embarrassed by Socrates because he is ignorant.

and sprocket. In this case, the ladder represents the stages on the divided line while the ultimate goal of the water is to travel to the Sun (the Good). However, as we noticed, there is a second force that is responsible for pushing the water onto the trough. This other force is the second turn that I have been at pains to articulate in this chapter. This turn away from the shadows of the cave provides impetus for the soul to carry out its desire.

If this metaphor is accurate, then *akrasia* is no longer an issue because weakness of will marks a divided soul. Both weakness of will and strength of will disappear in the individual who has self-control precisely because the individual is without conflict—the individual has perfected a manner of living such that he follows the path of knowledge as laid out by the dialectic, but is also compelled to do so because of a groundswell: a push that comes from the appetitive part of the soul.

Strength of will, at least as commonly understood, is also ruled out. I think most believe that strength of will denotes an individual who has strong inclinations to engage in some temptation and through a sheer act of will is able to resist acing on them. But if we equated self-control in Plato's sense with strength of will in the modern sense, then clearly such an equation would mean a decided impoverishment according to Plato. The harmonious individual is so well-aligned that even discord is part of his or her harmony.

Plato discusses this notion of natural control or rule in more detail where he writes:

> Then isn't to produce justice to establish the parts of the soul in a natural relation of control, one by another, while to produce injustice is to establish a relation of ruling and being ruled contrary to nature? Virtue seems, then, to be a kind of health, fine condition, and well-being of the soul, while vice is a disease shameful condition, and weakness.[34]

The most important part of this paragraph is the last line: "vice is a disease, a shameful condition and weakness." We are ashamed by our vices. It is this initial shamefulness, I argue, that initiates the dialogue in *The Republic*. Unbeknownst to the interlocutors, they are all being pushed to discover the truth of self-control, as it were, by an unknown force, namely, the shame they feel in being weak-willed.

"Therefore, dialectic is the only inquiry that travels this road towards the Forms because it does away with hypotheses and proceeds to the first

34. Plato, *The Republic*, 444d, 1076.

principle itself so as to be secure . . ." Plato writes on line 533c-d of *The Republic*.[35] However, if I am right, then it is not just the dialectic that is responsible for turning the eye of the soul towards the Forms when it is really "buried in a sort of barbaric bog."[36] Yes, the dialectic gently pulls the soul out of this aptly put "bog" and leads it upwards, but the crafts and techniques identified here in Book IX cooperate with the dialectic in terms of turning the soul around so as to reorient it. They serve to stimulate the initial push that the cave-dweller experiences to ascend to the Sun. Such practices remind the would-be-philosopher that the prizes, honors, and praises bestowed to those who are the sharpest at identifying the shadows that pass by the cave wall, are vacuous. There is no need to envy those who receive such awards.[37] All one has is the relationship one has to the self (the rapport a soi). All one possesses is one's sense of shame or conversely one's sense of self-approbation.

The question that I have been at pains to answer throughout much of this chapter and indeed throughout the entire book is the following: What does the dialectic hook onto in order to pull the soul upwards? I argue that it is the general sense of disgust and shame that the soul experiences immediately upon waking up from its deep slumber in the cave. It is this deep and disturbing undertow of emotion that allows the soul to turn away from the world of the shadows and to seek that which can dispel the fleeting narratives of temptation, namely the Sun.

There are important lessons to be learned from Plato's overall solution to the problem of *akrasia* as explained in his middle period. I will explain what these lessons are in the final chapter.

35. Plato, *The Republic*, 533c-d, 1149.
36. Plato, *The Republic*, 533d 1149.
37. Plato, *The Republic*, 516c-d, 1134.

Conclusion

Collapsing the Narrative of Temptation

THE SOUL TURNS TO that which is beyond all narratives, namely the light that illuminates all things: the Sun, the Good. The Sun Analogy disperses the clouds of narrative that plague the *akratic* individual: for the weak self is propped up by bad reasons. It dissolves the question raised in regard to Davidson's account of *akrasia* as explained in chapter one. If one recalls, that question was the following: How do we decide what is best, all things considered, when to consider any such thing is to always view it from some perspective, some agenda? What's more, since it is this agenda that provides the means and measures for the worth of the object in question, then how do we resolve the inner tension we experience when we feel that we are being torn apart by two very different narratives? This way of putting the matter is most accurate in my opinion. For is it not simply the case that we are being torn apart by two conflicting choices because each choice is infused with its own reason? Is it not the case that the temptation itself is indexed to a perspective, a mode of life presented to us by reason? How can one then measure the value of two contrary choices when the means of valuation is given by the narrative that comes to enframe each choice?

It is this profound insight that Socrates makes over and over again in *Protagoras*. Desires are not raw, Socrates teaches, they are infused with reason, and because they are so infused, desires are transmuted into interests. But Socrates thinking is mistaken for two reasons: (1) he believed that there was only one metric from which one can measure said interests; (2) he did not have a coherent answer to the question: Why do we measure? Why do we measure the value of competing interests?

Certainly several solutions to Socrates' problems are possible. One solution is to bridge what seemingly were once thought to be incommensurable paradigms. One way of doing this would be to secure a *rational* bridge from one agenda to the next. One might achieve this by further analyzing what it means to choose based on, "What is best all things considered?" Perhaps, upon further analysis, one might come up with a more fundamental ground that exposes the justification of a temptation, for example, as nothing more than a rationalization that is, in fact, upon closer analysis, not in keeping with one's true interests.

William Holton, for one, seems to adopt (albeit implicitly) this defensive stratagem. He claims that giving up one's considered resolutions too readily constitutes weakness of will. However, what very few commentators comment on is the qualifier "considered." For if one gives up his resolutions, but they are not considered, not deliberated resolutions, then, Holton argues, that individual is not weak-willed. At a minimum, the qualifier, "considered," is a necessary condition that an intention must satisfy in order for it to qualify as a candidate for a resolution. My question is this: What makes a resolution a *considered* resolution?

A considered resolution can only be made provided that one assesses not just what is under consideration, but what one considers to be worthy of consideration. But how does one decide that? What is worthy of consideration? Take an example that would be a paradigmatic example of a considered resolution, according to Holton. An agent, call him John, makes a resolution to wake up at 6am every morning to go for a run. He has very good reasons for making and committing to this resolution: he wants to be healthier, and running will improve his cardiovascular health. Also he knows that 6am is the only time that he can fit a workout into his schedule, etc. The resolution is a well-considered intention and John resolves to commit himself to implementing the resolution the next day. The following day, John wakes up, switches off his alarm at 6am, puts on his shoes, etc., but instead of running decides to spend an extra hour in bed. John never does run that day, nor does he run the next. He gives up on the resolution. In this case, Holton believes that John is weak-willed.[1]

So what then? How do we explain John's decision? To answer this question we must understand the deeper question surrounding *akrasia*: "What

1. See Holton, *Willing, Wanting, Waiting*, 122.

grounds consideration?" The answer cannot be: "further considerations" because then such a process would continue *ad infinitum* and would lead only to indecision and non-action. The alternative explanation, the one I am endorsing, is that there must be some affective ground that propels one to act. Reason can contour this initial non-rational impulse, but it has to work with what it has, or otherwise reason, all by itself, will not reach its desired aim. For Plato, this aim was to reunite with the Good; for my purposes, the goal of the self is to fulfill its work project: to reach and continue to cultivate a state of self-approbation. Without an emotional groundswell from "below" an individual cannot fulfill his or her work-project. This point can be further concretized by reflecting more carefully on both the *notion* and *act* of "considering."

If considerations simply grounded other considerations (e.g., whether I should take up running) then this well-considered intention must be grounded on considerations that I find to be self-grounding. But what makes such considerations self-grounding? Let's say I take up running because I wish to lose fat. This course of action has been recommended to me by my doctor and most people, I assume, might go about forming an intention to accommodate this recommendation. But notice that one could always go further and consider the following question in determining a course of action: "Why take up this recommendation?" The obvious answer is that by losing fat, I have a better chance of living longer. But again why is this preferable? If there are good reasons to think that living into my eighties, being warehoused in some nursing home, fills me with dread, then it is reasonable to reject my reasons for wanting to live longer. Indeed, a non-affective ground for understanding intention-based actions, *pace* Holton, leads to either indecisiveness or to an incoherent explanation as to why I act at all.

Intentions based on mere considerations are not enough to drive action; more than the act of "considering" is required when one makes a choice. To return to John the would-be jogger, when John is considering to take up jogging, his desire to form a considered resolution such that he will start jogging every morning at 6am, must ultimately originate from a non-consideration. When one reflects on the resolutions one has made in one's own life this point is obvious: resolutions are not just special intentions because they serve to defeat contrary inclinations. Resolutions are much more than that. If seriously made, they are last-ditch contracts one makes with oneself. They are often made in a time of shame and disgust. A time when one says, "I have to do something; I can't live like this any more!" As I have attempted to show, resolutions, or more generally work-projects, stem from two sources: a push from affective drives to overcome a particular behavior (or even perceived character flaw that the subject believes to be shameful) and a pull from an ideal relationship that one wishes to establish with oneself. As identified in chapter one, we all have work-projects: we instinctively desire to improve the current relationship we have to ourselves and to snuff out those relationships we already have which we believe to be harmful. Attempting to discover the ultimate rational pillars that undergird all narratives in order to act *enkratically* is impossible, so this project has shown. Rather one must be driven from the inside, as it were, to seek some alternative form of living that is conducive to self-approbation.

Plato's works have been instrumental in demonstrating this thesis. Plato is fully aware that a so-called "self-improvement project" based solely on well-reasoned considerations will not work. He discovers this or so I have argued in *Meno* and reverses the strong moral intellectualist position he affirmed in *Protagoras*. It is for this reason that Plato's solution to the problem of *akrasia*, as demonstrated in the middle period, is particularly instructive. To recap his answer, Plato first demonstrates, in *Phaedo*, that we experience ourselves as deeply furrowed entities: we are torn between two very different kinds of desires. But more than this, he reveals a deep-seated longing in the philosopher-type: a desire to return home, to be reunited with *Nous* (mind).

In *Symposium*, Plato then explains the source for this longing, namely, lack. It is this sense of lack that impels us to act. This impetus propels us to seek completion. Completion is arrived at when one knows and loves the Forms.

In Book IV of *The Republic* Plato extends his analysis further to show that there are three engines (reason, appetite, honor) within the soul, with each engine seeking to be whole, albeit using different means and methods. Each engine may be viewed as a mode of life. The mode of life will then determine which actions are to be pursued. These modes of life are much like narratives of action. They measure the worth of an action.

In Book IX, Plato measures each mode of life according to the litmus of pleasure. Even by stacking the deck in the favor of the individual who pursues pleasure, he shows that the philosophical life, the examined life, is the one most worth living and is the mode of life that should be pursued.

Plato then provides different means and strategies by which we can keep this insight as a guiding light throughout our long journey to wisdom.

What then is needed, according to Plato, in order to live a philosophical life? The answer is recognition: a recognition, if at first only dimly perceived, that reasons, evidence, argumentation to pursue the good are not enough. There must be a force that pushes us in the direction of the towline of the dialectic. Turning towards the tow-line is not something that everyone can do, or at least so argues Plato. This is not a debate I wish to enter. What is clear is that the journey from *akrasia* to self-harmony begins with a negative perturbation: it begins with a sense of dissatisfaction; a sense that whatever one pursues is never satisfactory. Pleasure is transient; knowledge based on the senses fleeting and identification with the body disappointing and anxiety producing. This dissatisfaction awakens a further call for completion: spiritually, epistemically, ontologically. For Plato, it is the Sun, understood as the Good, the stanchion beyond all Forms, that answers this cry of longing from the soul. For my purposes, the Sun is an analogue for self-approbation: we yearn to be one with our work-projects, for it is these work-projects that define the relationship we have to ourselves. As I have attempted to show in this chapter, the dialectic pulls one from this swamp of disappointment and disaffection towards the Sun. But the initial push to be towed, as it were, to turn towards the Forms stems from an affective push from below. Once the cave-dweller is so pushed and pulled, *akrasia* vanishes for the individual is no longer divided: gone are the weak and strong selves that Plato referred to in Book IV. All that is left is the project of completion.

Plato's work is important for my purposes because it shows how we must and can disperse the clouds of temptation in order to ascend to self-approbation. As I have argued, it is Plato's work that has served as my inspiration to discover how negative perturbations must be the well-springs that provide subjects with the driving force to heal the divisions within the *akratic* self. Once healed, a subject is no longer weak-willed; indeed, such a subject enjoys a new sense of ownership over his thoughts, actions, and feelings. Understanding *akrasia,* and overcoming it, can be resolved only if one considers and discovers the source of negative emotions, such as "agent-alienation," "caving," and so on. It is in the harnessing of these negative emotional "charges," along with the subsequent transmutation of them, that provide the impetus to becoming stronger, approbated individuals.

Bibliography

Abueita, Siham, and Hassan Lena Al Haj Mahmud. "Effectiveness of Expressive Therapy in Reducing Psychological Disorders, Improving Self-Esteem, and Social Support among Addicts." *Dirasat: Educational Sciences* 42.1 (2014) 139–61.

Ainslie, George. *Breakdown of Will.* Cambridge: Cambridge University Press, 2001.

Aristotle. *Nichomachean Ethics.* Translated by W. D. Ross. Oxford: Oxford University Press, 1988.

Augustine. *The Essential Augustine.* Edited by Vernon Joseph Bourke. Washington, DC: The Catholic University Press of America,1974.

———. *On Free Choice of the Will.* Translated by Thomas Williams. Indianapolis, IN: Hackett, 1994.

Aurelius, Marcus. *Meditations.* Translated by Martin Hammond. New York: Penguin, 2001.

Ayer, A. J. *Language, Truth and Logic.* 2nd ed. London: Golancz, 1946.

Bentham, Jeremy. *An Introduction to the Principles of Morals and Legislation.* 1823. Online: https://archive.org/details/anintroductionto2bentgoog

Bobonich, Christopher. *Plato's Utopia Recast.* Clarendon: Oxford, 2002.

Bratman, Michael. *Intentions, Plans and Practical Reasons.* Stanford, CA: CSLI Publications, 1999.

Camus, Albert. *The Stranger.* Translated by Matthew Ward. New York: Vintage, 1989.

Churchland, Paul. *Matter and Consciousness.* Cambridge: MIT Press, 1983.

Code, Lorraine. *Epistemic Responsibility.* Hanover, NH: University of Hannover Press, 1987.

Davidson, Donald. "How Is Weakness of the Will Possible?" In *Essays on Actions and Events: Philosophical Essays, Volume 1,* 21–42. Oxford: Oxford University Press, 2001.

Deleuze, Gilles, and Guatarri Felix. *Anti-Oedipus, Capitalism and Schizophrenia.* Translated by Robert Hurley. New York: University of Minnesota Press, 1977.

Descartes, René. *Meditations on First Philosophy.* In *René Descartes Meditations and Other Metaphysical Writings.* Translated by Desmond M. Clarke. New York: Penguin, 2000.

Dorter, Kenneth. *The Transformation of Plato's Republic.* Lanham, MD: Lexington, 2006.

———. "Weakness and Will in Plato's *Republic.*" In *Weakness of Will from Plato to the Present,* edited by Tobias Hoffman, 1–21. Washington DC: Catholic University of America Press, 2007.

Dreyfus, L. Hubert, and Paul Rabinow. *Michel Foucault, Beyond Structuralism and Hermeneutics. Second Edition with an Afterword by and Interview with Michel Foucault.* Chicago: University of Chicago Press, 1983.

Dyson, M. "Knowledge and Hedonism in Plato's Protagoras." *Journal of Hellenic Studies* 96 (1976) 32–45.

Elster, Jon. *Alchemies of the Mind.* Cambridge: Cambridge University Press, 1999.

Foeglin, R. "Three Platonic Analogies." *Philosophical Review* 80 (1971) 371–82.

Foucault, Michel. "An Aesthetics of Existence." In *Michel Foucault Politics, Philosophy, Culture Interviews and Other Writings, 1977–1984,* edited by Lawrence D. Kritzman, 47–57. New York: Routledge, 1988.

———. "The Ethic of Care for the Self as a Practice of Freedom." In *The Final Foucault,* edited by James Bernauer and David Rasmussen, 1–21. Cambridge: MIT Press, 1991.

———. *The History of Sexuality Volume II: The Use of Pleasure.* Translated by R. Hurley. New York: Random House, 1985.

———. "On The Genealogy of Ethics: An Overview of a Work in Progress." In *The Foucault Reader,* translated by Catharine Porter and edited by Paul Rabinow, 340–72. New York: Pantheon, 1990.

———. "What is Enlightenment?" In *The Foucault Reader,* translated by Catharine Porter and edited by Paul Rabinow, 31–50. New York: Pantheon, 1990.

Frankfurt, Harry. "Freedom of the Will and The Concept of a Person." *Journal of Philosophy* 68.1 (1971) 5–20.

———. *The Importance of What We Care About.* Cambridge: Cambridge University Press, 1988.

Freud, Sigmund. *Beyond the Pleasure Principle.* Translated by James Strachey. London: Hogarth, 1974.

Gordon, Jill. "Dialectic, Dialogue and Transformation of Self." *Philosophy and Rhetoric* 29.3 (1996) 259–78.

———. *Plato's Erotic World: From Cosmic Origins to Human Death.* Cambridge: Cambridge University Press, 2012.

Graves, Robert. *The Greek Myths.* London: Penguin, 1955.

Greco, John. "Virtues and Vices of Virtue Epistemology." *Canadian Journal of Philosophy* 23.3 (1993) 413–32.

Hackforth, R. "Hedonism in Plato's Protagoras." *Classical Quarterly* 22.1 (1928) 39–42.

Hernandez, L. "Chasing the High: A Firsthand Account of One Young Person's Experience with Substance Abuse." *Journal of Adolescent Research* 23.6 (2008) 770–73.

Heidegger, Martin. *Being and Time.* Translated by John Macquarrie and Edward Robinson. New York: Harper Row, 1962.

Hill, Thomas, E. "Kant on Weakness of Will." In *Weakness of Will from Plato to the Present,* edited by Tobias Hoffmann, 210–30. Washington, DC: Catholic University of America Press, 2008.

Hobbes, Thomas. *Of Liberty and Necessity.* Online: http://isites.harvard.edu/fs/docs/icb.topic1223571.files/hobbes%20on%20liberty.pdf

Holton, Richard. *Willing, Wanting, Waiting.* Oxford: Oxford University Press, 2009.

Homer. *The Odyssey,* Translated by W. H. D. Rouse. New York: Penguin, 1986.

Hume, David. *An Enquiry Concerning Human Understanding.* 1748. Indianapolis IN: Hackett, 1974.

———. *A Treatise of Human Nature.* 1738. Edited by David Fate Norton and Mary J. Norton. Oxford: Oxford University Press, 2002.

Kant, Immanuel. *Kant: Groundwork for the Metaphysics of Morals.* Oxford: Oxford University Press, 2003.

Kierkegaard, Søren. *The Sickness unto Death.* Translated by Walter Lowrie. Princeton, NJ: Princeton University Press, 1974.

Kurtzweil, Ray. *How to Create a Mind: The Secret of Human Thought Revealed.* New York: Viking, 2012.

Landry, Elaine. "Recollection and the Mathematician's Method in Plato's *Meno.*" *Philosophia Mathematica* 20.2 (2012) 143–67.

Lightbody, Brian. "Can we Truly Love That Which is Fleeting?" *The Florida Philosophical Review* 10.1 (2010) 25–42.

———. *Philosophical Genealogy: An Epistemological Reconstruction of Nietzsche and Foucault's Genealogical Method Vol. 1 and 2.* New York: Lang, 2010–11.

———. *The Problem of Naturalism: Analytic Perspectives, Continental Virtues.* Lanham MD: Lexington, 2013.

MacIntyre, Alasdair. *Whose Justice? Which Rationality?* London: Ducworth, 1988.

———. "Genealogies and Subversions." In *Nietzsche, Genealogy Morality: Essays on Nietzsche's Genealogy of Morals,* edited by Richard Schacht, 284–306. Berkeley: University of California Press, 1994.

McGonigal, Kelly. *The Willpower Instinct: How Self-Control Works, Why It Matters, and What You Can Do to Get More of it.* New York: Avery, 2012.

Mele, Alfred. *Backsliding.* New York: Oxford University Press, 2013.

Miller, Miller. "The Promethean Story in Plato's Protagoras." *Interpretation: A Journal of Political Theory* 7.2 (1978) 22–33.

Naas, Michael. "Philosophy Bound: The Fate of the Prometheus Socrates." *Research in Phenomenology* Winter (1995) 121–41.

Nietzsche, Friedrich. *The Gay Science.* Translated by Walter Kaufmann. New York: Vintage, 1974.

———. *On the Genealogy of Morals: A Polemic.* Translated by Walter Kaufmann. New York: Vintage, 1966.

Oxford English Dictionary. 10th ed. Oxford University Press: New York, 2002.

Perrin, Jacob. "A Defense of Socrates' Denial of Akrasia." *Dialogue: Journal of the Phi Sigma Tau Society* 54 1 (2011) 36–41.

Plato. *Apology.* In *The Great Dialogues of Plato,* translated by W. H. D. Rouse, 502–31. New York: Signet Classics, 1999.

———. *Euthyphro.* In *Plato Complete Works,* edited by John M. Cooper and translated by G. M. A. Grube, 1–16. Indianapolis, IN: Hackett, 1997.

———. *Meno.* In *The Great Dialogues of Plato,* translated by W. H. D. Rouse, 21–69. New York: Signet Classics, 1999.

———. *Phaedo.* In *The Great Dialogues of Plato,* translated by W. H. D. Rouse, 548–623. New York: Signet Classics, 1999.

———. *Philebus.* In *Plato Complete Works,* edited by John M. Cooper and translated by Dorothea Frede, 398–456. Indianapolis, IN: Hackett, 1997.

———. *Protagoras.* In *Plato Complete Works,* edited by John M. Cooper and translated by Stanley Lombardo and Karen Bell, 746–90. Indianapolis, IN: Hackett, 1997.

———. *Republic.* In *Plato Complete Works,* edited by John M. Cooper and translated by G. M. A. Grube and C. D. C. Reeve, 971–1223. Indianapolis, IN: Hackett, 1997.

———. *Symposium*. In *Plato Complete Works*, edited by John M. Cooper and translated by Alexander Nehamas and Paul Woodruff, 457–505. Indianapolis, IN: Hackett, 1997.

———. *Theaetetus*. In *Plato Complete Works*, edited by John M. Cooper and translated by M. J. Leavitt, and rev. Myles Burnyeat, 157–234. Indianapolis, IN: Hackett, 1997.

Pocket Oxford Greek-English Dictionary. Oxford: Oxford University Press, 2000.

Rawls, John. "Justice as Fairness: Political Not Metaphysical." *Philosophy and Public Affairs* 14 (1985) 223–51.

Rauhut, Nils Ch. *Ultimate Questions, Thinking about Philosophy*. 3rd ed. New York: Penguin, 2011.

Robison, Richard. *Plato's Early Dialectic*. Ithaca, NY: Columbia University Press, 1941.

———. "Plato's Separation of Reason and Desire." *Phronesis* 16 (1971) 38–48.

Sedley. D. "Teleology and Myth in the *Phaedo*." *Proceedings of the Boston Area Colloquium in Ancient Philosophy* 5 (1990) 359–83.

Silverman, Alan. "Plato's Middle Period Metaphysics and Epistemology." In *The Stanford Encyclopedia of Philosophy*. Online: http://plato.stanford.edu/entries/plato-metaphysics/

Sorabji, Richard. *Emotions and Peace of Mind*. New York: Oxford University Press, 2000.

Stalley, R. F. "Plato's Argument for the Division of the Reasoning and Appetitive Elements within the Soul." *Phronesis* 20.2 (1975) 110–28.

Stampe, Denis. "The Authority of Desire." *Philosophical Review* 96.3 (1987) 335–81.

Storr, Anthony. *Freud, A Very Short Introduction*. Oxford: Oxford University Press, 2003.

Teresi, Louis. *Hijacking the Brain: How Drug and Alcohol Addiction Hijacks Our Brains: The Science behind Twelve-Step Recovery*. Bloomington, IN: Authorhouse, 2011.

Vlastos, Gregory. *Platonic Studies*. Princeton, NJ: Princeton University Press, 1973.

———. *Socrates: Ironist and Moral Philosopher*. Cambridge: Cambridge University Press, 1991.

———. "Socratic Elenchus." *Oxford Studies in Ancient Philosophy* 1 (1983) 27–58.

White, N. P. *Plato on Knowledge and Reality*. Indianapolis, IN: Hackett, 1971.

Woolf, Ralph. "Consistency and Akrasia in Plato's Protagoras." *Phronesis* 47.3 (2002) 224–52.

Yi, R., A. E. Carter, et. al. "Restricted Psychological Horizon in Active Methamphetamine Users: Future, Past, Probability, and Social Discounting." *Behavioural Pharmacology* 23.4 (2012) 358–66.

Zagzebski, Linda. *Virtues of the Mind: An Inquiry into the Nature of Virtues and the Ethical Foundations of Knowledge*. New York: Cambridge University Press, 1996.

Zeyl, Donald, J. "Socrates and Hedonism. "Protagoras" 351b–358d." *Phronesis* 25.3 (1980) 250–69.

Subject Index

www.ingramcontent.com/pod-product-compliance
Lightning Source LLC
Chambersburg PA
CBHW050409030726
47503CB00006B/2097